It is instructive and pleasurable to read an important writer's formative work. These stories show the roots of Cheever's career and anticipate the fulfillment of his gifts. I am gratified that they are now conveniently available.

These stories are not literary curiosities; they are certainly worth rescuing from oblivion and worth republishing.

In particular, the stories written during the early Thirties have an objectivity of observation not always found in Depression fiction. They will stimulate Cheever's particular readership and will interest the celebrated mythical common reader.

—Matthew Bruccoli

THIRTEEN UNCOLLECTED STORIES
BY JOHN CHEEVER

THIRTEEN UNCOLLECTED STORIES BY JOHN CHEEVER

EDITED BY FRANKLIN H. DENNIS
INTRODUCTION BY GEORGE W. HUNT, S.J.

Academy Chicago Publishers

Published in 1994 by
Academy Chicago Publishers
363 West Erie Street
Chicago, IL 60610

Printed and bound in the USA on acid-free paper.
First Edition.

Library of Congress Cataloging-in-Publication Data

Cheever, John.
    [Short stories.   Selections]
    Thirteen uncollected stories by John Cheever /
edited by Franklin H. Dennis; introduction by George
Hunt.
    p.   cm.
    ISBN 0-89733-405-1 : $19.95
    I. Dennis, Franklin H.   II. Title.
PS3505.H6428A6   1994
813′ .52--dc20   93-49582
                                CIP

Contents

Editor's Note _____ i

Introduction _____ v

Fall River _____ 1

Late Gathering _____ 9

Bock Beer and
Bermuda Onions _____ 19

The Autobiography
of a Drummer _____ 37

In Passing _____ 45

Bayonne _____ 85

The Princess _____ 99

The Teaser _____ 111

His Young Wife _____ 121

Saratoga _____ 135

The Man She Loved ___ 163

Family Dinner_____ 189

The Opportunity _____ 201

THIRTEEN UNCOLLECTED STORIES
BY JOHN CHEEVER

Editor's Note

N 1979, *The Stories of John Cheever* received the Pulitzer Prize. To mark the publication of his omnibus, John Cheever wrote an elegant defense of the short story for *Newsweek* magazine. "Why I Write Short Stories" argued that the narrative "velocity" of the form—its speed at rendering events and character—best recorded "the newness in our ways of life... We are not a nomadic people," Cheever observed, "but there is more than a hint of this in our great country . . . so long as we are possessed by experience that is distinguished by its intensity and episodic nature, we will have the short story in our literature."

In that same article, John Cheever outlined a story using wryly observed elements of "Cheever country." His suburb—illusory rather than idealized— featured houses aping Elizabethan England

and the antebellum south. "Victorious domesticity" ruled the scene. One lawn even displayed a No Smoking sign.

Nowhere in the *Newsweek* piece did Cheever mention the Depression era, foreclosures, race track touts, waitresses in diners, bleak boarding houses, or revolutionary radicalism. But, in one of American literature's best kept secrets, John Cheever had made such subjects his concern and written about them memorably.

Although devotees of Cheever's celebrated "suburban fabulism" may react initially as if the stories from the '30s and '40s are reports from a foreign land, critics have long known and admired them. Scott Donaldson, Cheever's biographer, comments on the range of characterization in these stories:

> Time after time the economic crisis forces his characters to compromise their humanity and abandon their hopes. In evocations of the working class thought by latter-day critics to be beyond his ken, Cheever glimpsed the dreary and loveless lives of lunch-cart workers, striptease artists, and sailors down on their luck. More effectively his tales caught middle-class people trying to maintain their dignity in a time of diminished expectations.[1]

James E. O'Hara says that Cheever's narrative

instinct was compellingly apparent more than five decades ago, and his work "continued to display an uncanny ability to discover the hidden significance in seemingly unpromising material—everything from childhood dancing class to race track romance ... 'In Passing' ... offers persuasive evidence that Cheever at twenty-four could be remarkably sensitive to the political realities of the time."[2]

O'Hara ends his study by expressing the hope that the stories from the '30s and '40s

> will become more available to students and the reading public ... If and when that occurs, these people—the thoughtful audience that Cheever increasingly cherished as he grew older—will surely discover the full range of his storytelling abilities and his reputation as one of America's best storytellers can only grow as a result.[3]

Just as Cheever's celebrated novel *Falconer* plunged readers into the unexpected world of prison confinement, so many of the stories in this baker's dozen prove once again that Cheever's embrace of our "intense and episodic" experience is even more encompassing than we had thought.

Thirteen Uncollected Stories is arranged chronologically, and each story is annotated with the name and date of the publication in which it first appeared. The stories are reprinted exactly as they originally appeared, except that spellings and punctuation have been regularized in most cases.

Notes

[1] Scott Donaldson, *John Cheever: A Biography* (New York: Random House, 1988), p. 62.

[2] James Eugene O' Hara, *John Cheever: A Study of the Short Fiction* (Boston: Twayne Publishers, 1989), pp. 9-13.

[3] Ibid. p. 85.

Introduction

WHEN JOHN CHEEVER died in June 1982 at the age of seventy, his friend and fellow novelist John Updike composed a short, unsigned eulogy for *The New Yorker* magazine. Updike recalled that:

> One could not be with John Cheever for more than five minutes without seeing stories take shape: past embarrassments worked up with wonderful rapidity into fables, present surroundings made to pulse with sympathetic magic as he glanced around him and drawled a few startlingly concentrated words in that mannerly, rapid voice of his.

This present collection of thirteen hitherto uncollected stories allows us to watch what Updike described: stories take shape. But not that only: to watch a career take shape as well. For these stories provide a synoptic glimpse of his formative years, those efforts (as he called them) to discover his "singing voice," that assured, expansive, intensely personal style we associate with the mature Cheever of the 1950s and the 1960s.

With the exception of "The Opportunity" published in 1949, these stories date from 1931 (when Cheever was nineteen years old) up to 1942. Their settings and subject matter often correspond with his continual changes of residence during his impoverished Depression years. Thus we find three New England stories ("Fall River," "Late Gathering," "Bock Beer and Bermuda Onions") that reflect memories of vacations he and his older brother Fred took to New Hampshire and Cape Cod in the late 1920s and early 1930s. Two ("Autobiography of a Drummer" and "In Passing") recall memories of his visits home to Quincy, Massachusetts (a town near Boston, cf. "The Teaser") during the mid-1930s. There he had discovered that his salesman father had been laid off, his parents' marriage was crumbling fast, and the local bank was attempting to foreclose on the family home. From 1934 on (except for several months in 1939 when he stayed in Washington, D.C., working on WPA guidebooks), he lived in New York City—for a while in a dive near the Manhattan waterfront so dingy that the famous photographer Walker Evans immortalized its ambience in a photograph once featured in the Museum of Modern Art.

However, Cheever, an enthusiast for the outdoors and the "perfumes of life," like "sea water and the smoke of burning hemlock," was fortunate enough to escape the city for months at a time from 1934 on, after he applied and was accepted as a resident at Yaddo (where he became a favorite guest, owing to his wit and good manners). Frequent trips to the racetrack at Saratoga inspired three racetrack stories ("His Young Wife," "Saratoga," and "The Man She Loved"), all of which were published in *Collier's* magazine, an immensely popular (and well-paying) weekly that rivaled the then-reigning *Saturday Evening Post.*

I insert these biographical parallels with some trepidation, because Cheever himself was vehement about the oft-noted confusion between fiction and autobiography. In a 1976 interview, later published in the Stanford University literary review, *Sequoia,* he reiterated this objection by saying:

> What I usually say is, fiction is not crypto-autobiography: its *splendor* is that it is not autobiographical. Nor is it biographical. It is a

very rich complex of autobiography and biography, of information—factual information, spiri-
tual information, apprehension. It is the bringing
together of disparate elements into something
that corresponds to an aesthetic, a moral, a sense
of fitness.

Since so many Cheever stories, their characters
and circumstances seem to invite biographical interpretation, his protests often go unheeded. Nonetheless, they must be respected and understood.
For Cheever possessed what Wilfred Sheed called a
marvelous "mega-faculty," that interanimation of
memory and imagination which enabled him to
transform effortlessly any personal incident into a
magically altered story. Obversely, all his friends
agreed that any experience he underwent—unless
incorporated and transformed by his imagination—
simply ceased to exist for him. Hence, his resentment at crypto-autobiography.

I recall once going to dinner with Cheever and
being surprised when he gently complained that the
tables in the restaurant were too far apart. Puzzled,
I asked him why the disappointment, and he answered with a conspiratorial twinkle that "Now I
can't eavesdrop on any of the conversations." He
would regale friends by listening to snatches of

overheard remarks and, in an instant (as Updike alludes to), he could create a mini-story of intrigue, of randyness, of folly, about these unsuspecting diners that would have his dinner companions roaring with laughter. Everyone and everything he encountered was grist for a story, and he was ever at the ready. In this connection, he was once asked about the tools necessary for a novelist and he replied, "Well, it seems to me that virtually a perfect ear is as rudimentary to a novelist as his kidney, for example. That you have to be able to catch accents, to overhear what is being said four tables away. This is simply literary kindergarten as far as I am concerned." Needless to add, in this school Cheever became a post-graduate through an acceleration evident in these stories.

One autobiographical tale he did enjoy telling concerned the when and why of his writer's vocation. Its final version, embellished by a hint of suspense and some broad humor, went like this:

> I told my parents at age eleven that I wanted to be a writer, and they said they would think it over. In those days one went to one's parents for approval, hypocritically or otherwise. At the end of a couple of days, they said, 'Well, we've thought it over and we think it is perfectly

> all right if you want to be a writer, providing
> you do not pursue fame or wealth.' And I said I
> had no intention of becoming rich or famous.
> And they said, in that case, I could be a writer.

As for the reasons *why* he wrote, he admitted in a 1976 review that "I write at age sixty-six with precisely the same purpose as I did at sixteen which, of course, is to make sense of my life and perhaps to assist other people in making sense of their lives as fiction has helped me or continues to help me." In another interview not long before he died, he returned to his boyhood self and that boy's aspirations by ascribing it "to the fact that I found life immensely exciting. And the only way I had of comprehending it was in the form of storytelling."

These and similar remarks throughout his life make clear that Cheever never had hifalutin notions about his calling, nothing vaguely close to artists-as-the-supreme-legislators-of-the-world sort of hokum. Perhaps he loved literature in and for itself too much for that. At his most idealistic-sounding he could say that "Literature is the only continuous and coherent account of our struggle to be illustrious, a monument of aspiration, a vast pilgrimage" or "It seems to me only in literature

can we refresh our sense of possibility and nobility."
But these are isolated instances, usually reserved
for "grand" occasions. He was more likely to em-
phasize that "Literature is basic. The same language
that is used to describe a sunset can be used to buy a
pork chop." As for those stringent critical criteria
so prized by academics, he thought, instead, that
"the basic test of fiction is 'Is it interesting?' That's
the principal canon in writing—interest" and that
"interest connotes suspense, emotional involve-
ment and a sustained claim on one's attention."

No doubt Cheever's more modest claims for
literature derived from the fact that he himself
was, essentially, self-educated. Even after he had
attained considerable stature among writers, he
eschewed literary analysis of his own work and
that of others. He admired (and likely envied) his
estimable contemporaries, Saul Bellow and John
Updike, who could discuss fiction with an aca-
demic assurance, owing to excellent educations
that enhanced their diagnostic talents. Once I gin-
gerly raised the subject with him about critical
reservations regarding his novels because of their
lack of "architectonics" and organic shape (bluntly
put, the criticism of some that the novels were a

series of stories spliced together). Cheever smiled in a conspiratorial fashion and said, "Perhaps the reason is simple: I can't hold a long note as well as some others." And that was that—our lesson for today regarding analytic criticism.

The main reason for such reticence or reluctance is quite uncomplicated: John Cheever never graduated from high school. In later years, he would colorize the ignominy somewhat by claiming he was expelled "for smoking" or, more fancifully, "for seducing the son of the headmaster." The truth was more prosaic: his grades were abysmal. The prestigious Thayer Academy, the prep school he attended in Braintree, Massachusetts, tolerated his less than mediocre scholastic performance until the spring term of his junior year in 1930, when he was ousted without ceremony.

Cheever reacted in the way he knew best: he wrote a story about it, entitled "Expelled" and mailed it to *The New Republic,* then a popular left-wing weekly, that occasionally accepted short stories. "Expelled" was accepted, and a long literary career was launched. In addition, its submission ushered in a crucial association with Malcolm Cowley, the influential literary editor of *The New*

Republic, who was to become his quasi-mentor throughout the 1930s and whose contacts (along with those of the novelist Josephine Herbst) would later plunge Cheever into the social swim of literati like Sherwood Anderson, E. E. Cummings, John Dos Passos, Edmund Wilson and others of leftward tilt.

What Gertrude Stein said of another young writer, "He has the syrup, but it doesn't pour," could not be said of the eighteen-year-old Cheever. "Expelled" is a remarkably sure-handed piece, characterized by verbal economy and ironic wit. Its style is unabashedly Hemingwayesque, much like the tale of a prep-school Nick Adams. At this distance of over sixty years, it is important to recall the profound impression Ernest Hemingway's fiction made on budding writers throughout the 1920s. John Cheever, as a teenager, hungrily devoured the Nick Adams stories, *A Farewell to Arms* (1926), and the then-recent *The Sun Also Rises* (1929). Like so many others, he was held in thrall by Hemingway's style: its syntactical simplicity, its externalization of mood, its emotional restraint leading to effects created mainly through subtle implication rather than psychological exploration.

"Expelled" begins:

> It didn't come all at once. It took a long time.
> First I had a skirmish with the English depart-
> ment and then all the other departments. Pretty
> soon something had to be done. The first signs
> were cordialities on the part of the headmaster.
> He was never nice to anybody unless he was a
> football star, or hadn't paid his tuition, or was
> going to be expelled. That's how I knew.

Despite the narrative "I" here, the tone is flat and impersonal, the syntax is artificially simple, the cadence repetitive. The ominous vague "it" and "something" generate suspense by inference only, while our glimpse of the headmaster is glancing and impressionistic. But, right from the start, a reader senses he is in nimble-fingered hands.

The story "Fall River," which leads off this collection, is Cheever's second published story. It appeared in *The Left: A Quarterly Review of Radical and Experimental Art* in Autumn, 1931. The magazine's name boldly gives its game away, just as it effectively underlines Cheever's perspective in the story. *The Left* was an anti-capitalist journal, one of the many that blossomed and died early deaths during the Depression. Cheever's effort is essentially an elegiac description of a Massachusetts mill town, whose mills were closed by the plutocrats in Boston, as it is observed in gradual decay from winter to an (ironic) spring. Like "Expelled," "Fall River" provides a fascinating example of how a young writier could assimilate Hemingway's style and employ it for a different purpose. Take, for example, the story's second paragraph:

> The house we lived in was on a steep hill and we could look down into the salt marshes and the high gray river moving into the sea. It was winter but there had been no snow and for a whole season the roads were dusty and the sky was heavy and the trees had dropped their leaves for the winter. But the sky remained heavy and the roads were dusty for as long as three weeks and when the spring came it was hard to remember the snow because there had been so little.

For those who might be politically curious, Cheever's leftist sympathies were not long-lasting. During this period, his late teens and early twenties, he was for a time a member of the John Reed Club, and most of his literary acquaintances were devoutly left-wing. Nonetheless, although he remained a committed liberal throughout his long life (strongly anti-Fascist, suspicious of Big Brother intrusions), his personality and "conservative" respect for tradition, ceremony, Christian faith made him somewhat impervious to ideology. His interests were elsewhere: never in cosmic schemes for humankind but in the radical particulars of human life. His tilts of passion bent toward the moral and psychological and not the political.

This pilgrim's progress away from ideology is evident in the much longer short story included here, entitled "In Passing," and published in 1936 by *The Atlantic Monthly*. It is a sympathetic narrative, told in the first person by a young man and shaped through a series of richly observed sketches about several sets of people "down on their luck" (a refrain) during the Depression. As I mentioned earlier, much of this material corresponds with Cheever's and his family's straits at the time. Notable within it, however, is his deft portrait of the Communist organizer, whose presence takes on symbolic force throughout, in fact a counterforce of potential choice. When the narrator first hears him speaking at a church rally, we share his enthusiasm—until he adds an unsettling reflection by way of Hemingwayesque abstract nouns:

> He spoke for about an hour. He was a good speaker; his voice and his presence were attrac-

> tive and he could lift his voice until it filled the
> church. He still looked young and he gave the
> impression that he would never grow old, since
> he would never grow old through habit or love or
> vice.

A few days later, the narrator meets up with the organizer and has lunch with him. A passionate monologue ensues as "he talked and talked and talked" of revolution and the future dictatorship of the proletariat. The narrator summarizes the gist of his lengthy harangue in impersonal but not unsympathetic fashion, but then he suddenly (and slyly) tells us: "His voice, even when he spoke in hate, was precise and impersonal. He talked like a book; his talk had the clarity and dryness of a book. He ate slowly and uninterestedly."

Such lack of reverence on Cheever's part, even though gentle, did not endear him to his more committed acquaintances. In a 1977 interview with John Hersey, he explained further that "it seemed to me that the Communist Party attempted to take over, to direct, writing. Some people [I knew] decided that the only literature was the literature that would provoke social change. That struck me as being rubbish. And then, when I was perhaps twenty, I was singled out by Marxist critics in *New Masses* magazine as the final example of bourgeois degeneration. This more or less closed off any political relationships with the Communist Party."

Evidence, however, of Cheever's deeply personal, non-abstract contempt for the not-so-free enterprise system that brought on the tragedies of the Depression is found in the thinly-disguised narrative of his own father's career in "The Autobiography of a Drummer" (1935). Later, in his novel *The Wapshot Chronicle* (1957), he would recreate his father as that patriarchal figure of whimsical grandeur, Leander Wapshot, and recast his father's journals in an antic style, both hilarious and poignant. In this story, instead, we hear a direct, unadorned, confessional voice recount his history as a drummer (salesman) in an arc presaging Willy Loman's thirteen years later in Arthur Miller's *Death of a Salesman* (1948). It starts as a story of success, punctuated by train-rides ("Whenever I'm taking a train for another city it always seems as though my life were beginning"), and ends with him homebound ("The world that I know how to walk and talk and earn a living in, has gone"). The narrator's fate appears purely private until the final paragraph, where the pronoun "I" shifts suddenly to "we," and one hears: "We have been forgotten like those big yellow houses with cornices and cupolas that they used to build." Then suddenly another shift back to the "I," and an affecting admission that transcends every political philosophy closes the story.

Leftist ideologies might come and go, but Hemingway's melodies lingered on. Two stories, "Late Gathering" and "Bock Beer and Bermuda Onions," published in 1931 and 1932, retain the familiar voice right from their opening paragraphs. "Late Gathering" opens this way:

> It had rained hard early in August so the leaves were off the trees. In the sunlight the hills were like scorched pastry and when there was no sun the meadows were gray and the trees were black and the clean sky parted in firm lines down onto the smooth horizon. Most of the guests had gone away but some of the guests remained.

However, even in these two stories—and in a more pronounced fashion in the stories that follow—we happen upon comic contrasts, looser, more relaxed language and subtle, semi-lyrical repetitions that inch away from Hemingway's shadow. Cheever's lean, spare prose begins, gradually, to take on brighter colorations.

For example, in both these stories we find unexpected Joycean passages. In "Late Gathering" we happen upon this sentence amidst the Hemingwayesque inflections:

> Amy was in a corner talking to Jack and asking him not to bring down any more gin because down here it was not like in the city and in the city people could not stand the pace and it was all right to drink but down here there was a pace that people could adjust themselves to and there was no need of drinking and it was going to be one place where sensitive people could come and stand the realization of being sober.

Such comically ironic (in the context) experiments with Joyce as this run-on (and the Joycean use of dashes instead of quotes for dialogue, as in "Bock Beer and Bermuda Onions") are never found in Cheever's later stories. They stand out here as doffs of the hat to a writer he admired, and he would continue to insert playful tributes to others throughout his career.

What perhaps might be more surprising, however, to readers of Cheever's later stories, is how consistently woman-centered these early stories are. The familiar voice of the early Cheever is usually that of a narrator, unabashedly masculine in perspective, who is, by turns, doting, perplexed, poleaxed or dispirited by the profound mysteries of woman—and, if narrated in the third person, such is the condition of his central characters.

This intensely masculine perspective is absent here. Instead, for the most part we meet independent, self-assured women as central characters. These females are the most sympathetically observed of his central characters, they are given the best lines, endowed with genuine wit, and privy to the deepest sensations about life's mysteries. Even Mrs Dexter, the humorous centerpiece in the delightful "The Man She Loved" is a most genuine surprise. When we meet her at first, she seems the stereotypical scheming dowager, but by the end we root for her. And Cheever leads us toward compassion and admiration very skillfully:

> For all her chatting, her absentmindedness, her indiscriminate collecting of friends, no one, until then, could ever have accused Tilly Dexter of anything that was either comic or undignified. She was a woman who cherished her dignity, and now that she was destroying it, it was with great effort.

Tillie Dexter, Amy, Bayonne, Beatrice, Mrs Wilson, her "dumb" daughter, Elise—all remain fresh and rather unusual portraits in Cheever's gallery. And, needless to add, none of them resembles a Hemingway heroine.

Still there is no denying that Hemingway's influence on Cheever as a young writer was both salutary and incalculable. It encouraged extraordinary discipline in a writer, and imposed standards of simplicity and directness (qualities the mature writer retained). Unfortunately, the virtues of the style can easily degenerate into mannerisms and artificiality. Cheever intuitively sensed this limitation on himself, even though this realization never diminished his respect for Hemingway. In fact, one tale he loved to share was his encounter with Mary Hemingway, Ernest's last wife, who confided to him that her insomniac husband woke her from a sound sleep at three a.m. in November 1954, saying, "Wake up. I've just read this marvelous story called 'The Country Husband' by John Cheever and you've got to hear it," and he then proceeded to read aloud the whole densely plotted story to her at her bedside.

Years later Cheever recalled his predicament at

the time, saying, "I think one has the choice with imagery, either to enlarge or diminish. At this point (1976) I find diminishment deplorable. When I was younger I thought it brilliant." He then addressed this realization in terms of the treatment of fictional characters: "The proper function of writing, if possible, is to enlarge people, to give them their risk, if possible to give them their divinity, not to cut them down." In short, the Hemingway model was inhibiting his creative energies. Gradually, "enlargement" becomes the key to his later style. His fellow feeling toward the reader becomes more expansive, his narrative voice more comfortable and relaxed and less distant in tone. This process of enlargement will finally bloom into the myth-inhabited, fantastical world that becomes his distinctive "Cheeveresque" fiction a decade and a half later.

So, the restless neophyte had to look elsewhere for stylistic interpretation, and he found it in F. Scott Fitzgerald. Fitzgerald's *Tender is the Night* appeared in 1933, rekindling interest in his earlier stories and *The Great Gatsby* for Cheever and other writers. Fitzgerald's inspiration liberated Cheever's romantic instincts and nostalgic sensibilities, and it encouraged him "to dignify the trivial while remaining fairly ironic toward it" (as critic Kenneth Elbe said of Fitzgerald). This influence is evident immediately in such skillful character-sketches or profiles, as "Bayonne," "The Teaser," and "The Princess," all of which were published in 1936-7. In each of these stories, we encounter a series of dramatic scenes wherein characters stand revealed through dialogue, *sans* narrative comment. The writers' concern is with exact verisimilar dialogue and speech patterns, in such a way that the stories become "playlets" rather than narratives— so characteristic of Fitzgerald's fiction. The five stories that close this volume demonstrate the gradual "enlargement" he eagerly sought.

For example, such "enlargement" is evident in the opening lines of each of these stories. Each begins boldly with a story-teller's assurance, alerting the reader to suspicions of what might follow:

"His Young Wife" begins:

> When John Hollis married a young girl he was probably the only one who was conscious of the difference in their ages. Sue was too young and impulsive to be conscious of anything like that and, anyway, in the beginning they were very happy together.

In two brief sentences we sense the story's kernel. The deliberate repetition of words like "young" and "conscious" prompt our attention, as we puzzle over that "anyway" and "in the beginning." Thus the story's shape is framed immediately.

"Saratoga" begins:

> When Roger Gaige came down to the track that morning and told everyone, the trainers, the stableboys and railbirds, that he was going to change his way of living, a lot of them laughed openly and MaGrath, his best friend, couldn't conceal a smile.

Most writers would avoid a lengthy, casually-phrased temporal clause to open a story, so we sense this choice must be deliberate. Why? Does that "When" and what follows hint at a temporal regularity (perhaps repeated overmuch) to Roger's announcement? Why the universal laugh and the semi-concealed smile? And why the leisurely, almost lazy pacing of the sentence? Could Roger be a lazy recidivist? So, the story.

"The Man She Loved," unlike the two above, does not open with a detailed temporal clause. Instead, it begins with a glimpsed scene, wherein we catch the characters exposed despite themselves. The narrator's voice is direct, pointed, but non-informative. In this way he "enlarges" his characters and reduces his own role to an "I am a Camera" spectator.

> Mrs Dexter overheard Joe ordering a pork chop. That was the way it began. The Dexters were late in going up to the diner and all of the tables were taken. The waiter gave them three unoccupied chairs at Joe's table. They nodded to Joe in the way that strangers nod to one another in a dining car and then everybody sat down and stared at the menu. The waiter returned a few minutes later and Joe ordered a pork chop. "But, young man, you shouldn't eat pork," Mrs Dexter told him, "you don't look at all well and you shouldn't eat pork— fried pork."

In this story and those following, Cheever seems less hurried, more confident about the reader's patience and intelligence, and less concerned about informing him of essential data right off the mark. In short, he lets the pork chop do the work for him, by establishing the setting and the "taste" of his characters before the action proper starts. In "The Family Dinner," he modifies this technique of scene-setting in starker terms and, instead of identifying the characters by name, he introduces them with the deliberately upsetting "He" and "She" merely. This device, complemented by the alternating of short and long phrases, creates suspense— totally unexpected, given the story's homey title.

> He was there first, a thing that was to be expected. The weekend crowds had gone and had not yet begun to return and there were only a few soldiers in that part of the railroad station that resembles the Baths of Caracalla. He was early; she was on time and at a quarter to one he saw her coming down the escalator. I have never seen her before—he thought—I am a stranger, a drummer waiting for a Baltimore train and is she worth watching or isn't she?

That last sentence, a privileged entry into the mind of a character, reveals a technique that Cheever will exploit and refine in his later fiction. The narrator offers us direct access into a character's thoughts, but even the word "thought" puts us on our guard. Are such thoughts mistaken or correct? Are they really thoughts or just surmises on the part of the narrator? The last story in this collection, "The Oppportunity," teases us designedly, tantalizing us into puzzling about appearances vs. reality and what "thinking" actually means. The story opens:

> Mrs Wilson sometimes thought that her daughter Elise was dumb. Elise was her only daughter, her only child, but Mrs Wilson was not so blinded by love that the idea that Elise might be stupid did not occasionally cross her mind. . . . She was a beautiful girl with dark hair and a discreet and striking grace, but Mrs Wilson sometimes thought sadly that there was a discrepancy between Elise's handsome brow and what went on behind it. Her face and her grace were almost never matched by anything she had to say. She would sit for an hour at the end of her bed, staring at nothing. "What are you thinking about?" Mrs Wilson would ask; "What's on your mind, Elise?" Elise's answer, when she made it, was always the same. "Nothing. I don't know. I wasn't thinking about anything."

The comic eye of Cheever, so familiar to readers of his later fiction, is peeping out here by way of a droll voice, caught merely observing a family scene. The effect is so simple that one realizes, only on reflection, how calculated it is and how gracefully it has been achieved. All five of these last stories end in surprise, but the truer surprise lies in the dexterity that has led us to it.

In 1965, Cheever was invited to contribute a short biography of Fitzgerald to the anthology entitled

Atlantic Brief Lives. His essay points up those very qualities he himself assimilated during the thirties and incorporated into the later stories we find in this collection. He says of Fitzgerald's stories:

> these are not rueful vignettes or overheard conversations but real stories with characters, invention, scenery and moral conviction.... The best of these stories were lived as well as written—an irreversible process that sometimes ends in grief, but he remained astonishingly hopeful.

Those last sentences sound eerily self-revelatory as well. What's more, Cheever's concluding tribute to Fitzgerald reads like a professor's prelection on how to appreciate Cheever's own fictional aims:

> Great writers are profoundly immersed in their time and he was a peerless historian. In Fitzgerald there is a thrilling sense of knowing exactly where one is—the city, the resort, the hotel, the decade and the time of day. His greatest innovation was to use social custom, clothing, overheard music, not as history but as an expression of the meaning of time. All the girls in their short skirts and those German tangos and the hot nights belong to history, but their finest purpose is to evoke the excitement of being alive. He gives one vividly the sense that the Crash and the Jazz Age were without precedent,

but one sees that this is part of his art and while Amory, Dick, Gatsby, Anson—all of them—lived in a temporal crisis of nostalgia and change, they were deeply involved in the universality of love and suffering.

Cheever's own words—with slight alteration, at most—provide the finest introduction to the thirteen stories in this collection.

George W. Hunt, S.J.
New York,
November, 1993

Fall River

PEOPLE HAD KNOWN it for two years but it was obvious in the winter. The mills had stopped and the great wheels were still against the ceilings. The looms blocked off the floor like discarded machinery in an old opera house. On the floors and on the beams and on the brilliant flanks of steel the mist of the web was covered with dust like old snow.

The house we lived in was on a steep hill and we could look down into the salt marshes and the high gray river moving into the sea. It was winter but there had been no snow and for a whole season the roads were dusty and the sky was heavy and the trees had dropped their leaves for the winter. But the sky remained heavy and the roads were dusty for as long as three weeks and when the spring came it was hard to remember the snow because there had been so little.

The dark city grew up from the river and all winter the spires of the wooden church were held up against the sky like enormous fingers. From our window we could see the piles of the hill out of the river and the dirty houses blown with smoke and blousy with sunlight. We had known it for almost a year now and the people had spoken of a dry winter. It was already spring. The full river moved into the ocean. The great wheels of the machinery were still waiting against the ceiling. The round stacks shot out into the sky vacant without the dark plumes of smoke.

Our room was on the fourth floor of a high brick house. A great many people could not pay their rent and the landlady made the silence miserable with her complaints. There was a man on the third floor who had a job and who earned ten dollars a week. In the evenings we would see him sitting on the edge of his bed looking slowly about the empty room. The landlady would weep when she saw him and tell him that she must eat and that he must pay his rent. That he would have to pay his rent. The man's face was square and his hair was straight like plain wood. You will have to pay the rent, the landlady shouted on the small landing outside of his door. He looked at her and closed the door gently. I will pay you the rent next week. His mind was confused with the impossibility of his debt. With the broken face of the landlady shouting for her rent.

We had not paid our rent for three weeks but it was different when there were two people. We had sent our books away in big boxes a month ago. These were things that we did not want to do but even in this building of steep brick the people were not the same. The landlady would have taken our books and our typewriter and sold them. Cigarettes were not safe if you left them on the table for a minute.

An old man downstairs had been out of the mill for six months now. At first he could not stand the leisure and he was up every morning going across the river to the city looking for work. When he found that there was no work he was still up every morning walking over the city all day and coming back across the great river at night talking to the men who did work. He had been that way for two months and then he fell and hurt his leg. When his leg was better he had lost all his desire to walk. He only left his room to buy food and to return and eat it. You could see that when the wheels began to turn and the long bands quivered with the sharp motion he would not go back. He was living in his room, going out to buy food and coming back again. No one knew what he did in his room all day. You could not hear him move.

People had admitted a dry winter with very little money and no food. It had been this way. The winter had come and gone. The factories were still vacant. The river was moving always but there was no smoke over the city. Half the town was still out of work. The river and the seasons came and went but the machinery was quiet and we did not know when it was going to move again.

In the north there were great empty boats resting in the harbors waiting for a cargo. They were chained away from the docks and they moved back and forth with the currents of the tide. We had seen them in the summer and if we went back in the spring we knew that they would still be there. Enormous piles of steel and glass turning on the tide and waiting for a cargo. It would not be this spring or perhaps it would not be even in the summer. The boats would still wait on the harbor resting with one light in the dark warm evenings.

If people had mentioned and realized a dry winter they did not talk about the spring. There was no reason why they should mention the spring. The factories were still idle. The boats were vacant in the northern harbors and there was still very little money and no food. In the east the workers had complained and the drums and the pickets and the sound of their complaint in the fine rain was like thunder beneath the hills. The church had stopped it. The church had quieted it but it had not stopped the thunder. The workers were still dissatisfied and in the fine rain they remembered their complaint and the sound of their drums. There were few who could forget the sound of the *Internationale* and although in the east the wheels were moving again they were moving under a stranger master. They were waiting for hands that knew them and the ways to control their levers.

From our window we could see the spring come because we had a great deal of time. At first it was the delicate air and the sweet stink of the oil vats from across the river. Then the trees were dusty with new buds and the old gardens were pushed away and the river was carrying sticks of bright wood and waste that had come down in the thaw. The sky was heavy like flesh and there was no doubt about the spring. We could see it clearly in the hills that were thawing and the sore pain of the broken earth. And yet the wheels were not moving and the looms were still like nervous dancers and there were very few people who wanted to talk about the spring because of these things.

In Boston the wealthy people were nervous. It was spring but it would make no difference. They were terrified at the possibility of having to live through another season. Of having struggled through the winter searching for the pleasures of previous winters. In Boston the wealthy people were conditioned like old gentlemen. The nervous wreckage of a dead race. It was wrong to accuse them of injustice. They could not accustom themselves to the new necessities. They were nervously fumbling, handling enormous conditions that had been thrust into their hands. And the other people were waiting for them to drop these things. Perhaps the machines would start again by the summer but they would still be under foreign control. Perhaps they would go on for a whole year while there was unrest like thunder under the hills. There would be something. Nobody who had seen the things come and the things go could doubt that. We were watching the spring pass like a great tide up the river and down over the hills.

On Sunday Paul came in his new shiny car and took us out to the farm. Paul was prosperous and his business was doing well. He showed us the speed of his car and the splendid little wheels that turned beneath the hood. Then we went down the long planes of the country road and circled the enormous gravel driveway. The large white farmhouse with the river on its left and the orchards running to the river was the same. Mani came to the door in a long pale dress and took us out to her flower garden. There were firm yellow sprouts breaking through the hard earth. Mani swore a little and said that it was spring. The sky was heavy. The birds were crossing it like a high dome. At the end of the river the mills were still and the boats were shifting on the tide waiting for a cargo. Mani said that it was spring again and stamped her cigarette out on the edge of the garden. It is spring again, Mani said.

The Left:
A Quarterly Review of Radical and Experimental Art.
Autumn, 1931

Late Gathering

I T HAD RAINED hard early in August so the leaves were off all the trees. In the sunlight the hills were like scorched pastry and when there was no sun the meadows were gray and the trees were black and the clean sky parted in firm lines down onto the smooth horizon. Most of the guests had gone away but some of the guests remained.

In the evening Richard and Fred walked down to the formal pond in the sand pit and watched the swans drift in the wind. Richard woke early every morning and looked at the hills. Then he shook off his pyjamas and caught his body swinging past the glass panes in the small window. His body was a lined angular whiteness passing the small panes in the window when he was not looking.

Fred did not get up until noon and the sun was hot on the roofs or the rain had stopped and the foliage was brittle with water. The coals in the small hearth were black and he had to heat his coffee. Amy told him that if he would come down sooner he would not have to drink cold coffee. Amy ran her eyes down the length of red carpet and laughed like a gramophone. Some of the guests were walking up and down the verandah wondering if it were going to rain, and the ducks came out of the gray shed and went to the small pool in the bottom of the sand pit.

A lady with a staff of black hair pulled back from her forehead and broken over the round of her skull spent most of the afternoons and a great many of the evenings eating sandwiches and telling everyone how beautiful Switzerland was.

"You have never really seen the fields I have. You do not know what a flowered meadow is. You have never walked into fields that were blue and white and yellow and every flower as perfect as the nipples on your breast. Curved just so, colored so lightly, and you have never heard the sound of running water. Oh no, you have never heard the sound of running water.

"You have never lived by a little stream that

made a sound all day and all night. You do not know what it is to go away and not hear the little stream any more. It is like silence to you. Yes, it is like silence to you.

"And the stars? No. You do not know what stars are like. You have never been near enough to the stars to see the long streaming continuation of one line into another. You have never been so high that from your verandah the birds were like level wheels in the meadow and the meadows like patches of juniper. Oh no. You do not know. Enormous meadows like mere patches of juniper up on the hillside where there are no trees.

"And perhaps you have lived so high on a hill that the mist came up from the patched meadows like a pitted fruit and gathered in circles and little whirlpools? You have never seen a thick mist stream through the doorway and flatten on the ceiling." She would tap her foot on the flowered linoleum and lift up the corner of a sandwich. "You do not know how enormous things can be and I am afraid that you will never know."

Fred and Richard went for walks together in the hills and often stayed all day. They took their books and sandwiches and sometimes bread and cheese and bad wine. They bent their backs over the round of the hill and watched the clouds and, when there were no clouds, the trees break along the wind. There was no need of speaking. A gramophone was a great responsibility. Resting on their backs against the flank of a broken hill they instinctively felt that the silence was going to lapse into the scratching of a gramophone needle and someone would have to crank the machine. There was an enormous responsibility in choosing one side or another of the disk.

Sitting on the top of the hill they could see Amy lean from the cross windows and shout at the cows. The foliage was dead and the flagpole had been taken down because of the strong wind. In the long vacant drawing room the stiff twigs of the bridal veil* pulled and scuttled over the clean glass.

On the other side they could see hills dropping onto hills dropping into the ocean. They could see Chestnut Hill and Break Hill ram one another and push the small scrub pines down

* This is probably a reference to "bridal wreath", a flowering bush of the *spiraea* family. —Ed.

over the beach. In the empty weather when there was no sun they could hear the ocean make a great noise on the rocks and speculate on the color and the formation of the waves. Often they did not know how they spent whole days in the hills lying on the sharp grass wondering about one another.

Amy said the Russian lady with the broken hair had never been to Switzerland but that she had seen a great many milk chocolate advertisements. Amy said that the Russian lady with the vacant eyes was simply waiting for her son to come from a college out west and take her back to Cambridge. People began to wonder if she even had a son who was coming from out of the west to take her back to Cambridge. She sat in her black brocade pyjamas on the verandah and described the milk chocolate advertisements and everyone listened to her because she was so very, very beautiful.

In the delicate light of the early evening Fred and Richard came down from out of the hills and said good afternoon to everyone. Fred traced a white iris with the toe of his boot on the flowered linoleum. Richard bent over the whitewashed railing and said how beautiful everything was. Amy was in the corner talking to Jack and asking him not to bring down any more gin because she didn't like to start drinking down here because down here it was not like in the city and in the city people could not stand the pace and it was all right to drink but down here there was a pace that people could adjust themselves to and there was no need of drinking and it was going to be one place where sensitive people could come and stand the realization of being sober.

When Ruth played the piano it was very nice also and Fred and Richard dusted the white-wash from their trousers and stood close to one another listening to the music roll out of the doorway and heave over the stubble of unkempt lawn. Because the leafless trees made it look much later in the season than it really was, the awning had been taken down from the verandah and the black metal skeleton shot off the roof and hung between the floor and the railing like a vacant elbow. Such muscle in the awning frame Ruth would say and drag her fingers over the dry ivory like little white rakes.

Fred and Richard felt that a clock was running

down somewhere and that someone would have to wind up the clock in a little while. Amy sat on the blue wooden balcony with Jack and talked about how fine and lovely everything had been before people started to go to the city and get drunk.

"People who used to come out here eight years ago and find the place restful now want to get drunk after their first meal. They find the tempo of nature almost more unbearable than the tempo of New York. Instead of finding rest in the country they become nervous wrecks. I do not understand it, no I do not understand it."

When Richard undressed, his body was warm like a well-lit room and he spent a lot of time jumping up and down before the oval mirror. He could hear Fred walking down the corridor in his leather slippers and he crossed his legs and lit a cigarette. Fred came in and said good night and went away again. Richard noticed sharp colors, brilliant shadows and the manner in which the boards were placed in the floor. He remembered a great many numbered forms and objects with names on them so that he could tell them that it was half past eleven when the

Huntington Avenue trolley car crashed into the one roaring down Massachusetts Avenue in the direction of the river. In this way he went to sleep and often when he dressed in the morning it was raining and the window was running with the ugly shapes of flat water.

Ruth got a letter from her brother at the farm saying that he would have to close up because the deer had destroyed whole sections of his orchard. Fred thought it was all very beautiful with the slender arched animals eating the delicate boughs and Amy put on an evening gown and came down to supper after everyone had been working all day.

There were so few guests now that they could all be seated in the dining room and Amy carved the roast at the table. Everyone talked and the meat fell away under the knife. In the dining room the curtains had not been hung yet but someone had started to put back the pictures on the yellow plaster. Amy asked Richard if he would have more meat and looked out of the window. It would be a month now and the dry snows would be coming in from the frozen harbor. Then she remembered that it was not as late as she thought it was but that the rain had driven the leaves from the trees and it was really only the beginning of the autumn.

In the middle of the meal a car came up the drive and Amy rose in her ball dress and ran to the door. A lot of people came in and she kissed them and took their coats off. Then they sat down at the table and she was busy carving the meat and keeping the coffee percolators full.

That night Amy told Richard that there were not enough beds and that he would either have to sleep with Fred or go out to the bungalow. The Russian lady told him that he had better sleep in the bungalow and he said that he would sleep in the bungalow.

Amy wrote her name on the window and kept reminding herself that it really was only the beginning of autumn even if the trees were bare.

Pagany
October-December, 1931

Bock Beer and Bermuda Onions

THE INDIANS COME in on a late Sunday afternoon and they leave on the following Thursday. The weather is turning gradually from winter into spring. There are a great many guests at the farm, some planning to stay through the spring into the summer, and a few who have come down from the city for the weekend. The bedrooms are crowded and disturbed until the house looks like a hotel, and Amy is tired of being a hostess to so many people. From her bedroom she can hear them playing the gramophone and shouting out their card numbers. When the Indians come in she is sitting alone in her bedroom looking out of the window into the gardens.

They come and go with incredible rapidity and quiet. No one knows who they are when they come and they know less when they have gone.

While they are camped in the meadow the weather completes a final change. The air is sweet and unlocked. The gardens and the fields go finally green. The river is so high with the thaw that it cannot be any higher. The sky is sky. The trees are trees. Amy sits alone in her bedroom rocking back and forth in her chair. She will have her forty-fifth birthday on the second of April. It is still March, but the warm wind makes April very near. She gets up and looks at herself in the mirror and counts her wrinkles. Then she sits down again and rocks back and forth looking out of the window and thinking about her age. It is impossible to comprehend forty-five springs, and the forty-fifth will be as much of a failure as the others. One can lose a husband in the war, she is thinking, and open a house in the country and spend on thirty guests the substance one would have given to a husband. But a house full of guests and memory crowded with spring only makes the sum of her, flesh, blood, wrinkles, hair, a more final object to go up against April. She is aware of the ticking of every clock, the dripping of every gutter. She is aware of the passing of day and light, morning, afternoon, the

confusion of twilight, evening. She is aware of
the spring and the changes in the season. There
is a swift ripple of green, fashioned from wheat
between the two vegetable gardens. A terrible
green that has trickled into the landscape like
cold water. The river is full. The rains will be
warm and bitter hammering at the tin roof. And
she cannot hold this back. Her hands are flesh-
less and nervous, strident with strange energy.
She cannot put them up and make it ageless and
changeless and winter forever. She cannot hold
this back with her hands any more than she can
dam a cataract or a great wave.

Five people are playing lotto in the drawing
room. Mrs White, her daughter, Rachel, Peter.
Someone in the dining room is playing one of
the gramophone records. It is an old record
warped and distorted with use. The music comes
out in bunches, the voice trembles and sings. A
thin voice with a shallow throat that seems to be
choked way forward in the mouth. The trom-
bones flower and blare. The beat is rapid, swifter
than the falling of water. Amy taps her feet on
the floor in time to the music and thinks about her
forty-fifth April and the great symbol and seal of

spring as Bock beer and Bermuda onions. She can hear Rachel laugh and beat the card table. Mrs White's short-postured laughter. Peter's growling. Rachel stamps the floor and beats the card table, this time overcome with laughter.

Then a big maroon sedan comes up the driveway and parks by the front door. Two men get out of the car and walk over the lawn to the steps. Rachel gets up from the card table and meets them at the door.

—Hello, she says. Is there anything I can do for you?

The men look her over. One of them wears a gaudy necktie as lurid and terrible as metal.

—We want to see Mrs Henderson, he says.

Rachel goes out of the room into the corridor and shouts up the stairwell. Amy comes out of her bedroom and walks down the staircase. She moves proudly and nervously across the room to the two men standing in the door frame against the twilight. They are both dark with black empty eyes and thin, pinched faces, either Mexican or American Indians.

—Hello. Amy laughs and wraps her jacket around her.

—Are you Mrs Henderson?

—Why yes. She laughs again.

—We asked at the store, the first one says, and they said you have a large meadow where we could camp if we would pay you rent. We are a tribe of Cherokee Indians. There are twenty of us. We have our tents, and all we will do will be to camp in the meadow. This man is the chief. His name is Mario.

The second man steps forward. He is dark and slow with a strange coolness to his person. He speaks in careful broken English:

—I am the chief. We will be very clean. We will only stay one week and we will pay you five dollars. We will not leave any papers and we will be careful of our fire.

Amy laughs again.

—But I don't know anything about you, she says. This is a private farm. Will you make much noise? Will you guarantee me the five dollars?

The first man speaks again. The chief puts a stick of gum in his mouth and chews rapidly.

—We are Cherokee Indians from a Government reservation in Oklahoma. We will pay you five dollars in the middle of the week. We are very quiet.

Amy turns and looks at the other people in the room. Then she shrugs her shoulders and ends her sentence in a question.

—All right. You can stay. But don't camp beyond the fence. She turns around and walks over to the card table. The two Indians go down the front staircase without speaking to one another. It is getting dark. The twilight changes and turns with the security of a merry-go-round coming to a halt. Amy puts on a sweater and walks back and forth in the room talking to the people who are playing cards. We will have Indians at the farm too, she says. Maybe they will do war dances and paint their faces for us. I think that they must be a hoax. What would Indians be doing in this part of the country in the spring? They are probably very shrewd gypsies. But we have had everything, why shouldn't we have Indians.

Within an hour four cars drive up and park in the meadow. Six tents are lifted and a fire is built. Amy stands on the verandah watching the small fire fastened between the two hills. She watches the forms shift closely around the flame, black padded movements, elegant, silent gestures. She cannot hear them talk. Only the sound of the women's bass laughter. The evening air is warm. The curtains are flapping. All she can think of is Bock beer and Bermuda onions.

There is a strange forgotten blood bond between these two exact types of Americans. The influence of the landscape is secret and beyond control. The first have erected their tents on the soil between the hills. The second have built these strange white farmhouses that look like deflowered temples in a violated wilderness. And it is with this half interest that Amy goes down to the camp fire with her guests, to question and examine the Indians.

The first impulse is to hate them for their control and quiet and pride. At first because of the women's costumes, the exactness of gesture, the warmth of their language, Amy and her guests carry on a deliberate unspoken warfare of hate and indifference. But the Indians are very convincing as Indians and they can weave flowers out of straw and roll cigarettes with one hand and do tribal dances and sing songs if they are given gin in payment. When the first impulsive indifference has been spent, Amy and her guests sit down at the camp fire among the Indians and ask and answer questions. The chief tells them that they are traveling around northern New York and New England. They will do this until autumn, when they go back to Oklahoma. Amy explains her existence. The facts that she is childless, that her husband was lost in the war, that she lives alone on this farm with a shifting mass of friends to defend her from loneliness. The Indians are interested in her aloneness and want to know how much she will sell the farm for, and are the floors in good condition. They quibble with one another over the condition of the floors.

There is an older man in the group, who drinks too much and then laments the passing of his race. His face has sagged, his eyes are loose and heavy. When Amy brings him a half a pint of gin and a package of cigarettes he tells them the myth of creation. The other Indians watch him and tolerate him with a quiet patience. The women are stout and smooth like a type of southern Jew. They wear great muslin skirts of lilac and yellow that hang to the ground. Their breasts and blouses are ornamented with coins and pendant drips of imitation gold and silver. While the old man tells the myth they lean close to the flame, their jewelry rattles, they talk to one another in simple bunches of language. The myth is great, but it is imperfectly told by this half-intoxicated Indian. The greatness has become incidental. It is something of incredible weight being passed carelessly from tongue to tongue. The old man's face is draped and toothless, pinched up with gin. But while he talks an inner brilliance is imposed on his features. He can remember his own superiority, his secret faith in the Messiah of the feathered serpent locked between the waves of a lake and yet greater than all the lakes in America, than all the lakes and rivers and mountains. The great feathered serpent locked between soil and water, deathless and terrible, more terrible than the sum of all the soil and water that shelters him.

The old man tips the gin bottle up to his lips and then pushes it down again into the warm spring soil. When he talks he rocks back and forth. He belches and fumbles with his cigarette and tries to summon words and phrases out of his memory. The other Indians talk among themselves all the time. Talk and chew gum and light cigarettes.

In the beginning it was all ocean with nothing but a high place. The animals lived in the high place and there were many and it was crowded. They sent the beaver down onto the water and he discovered mud which he brought to the surface. The mud grew and spread until it formed an island. Later the island was fastened to the sky by four great cords. The sky is a vault of stone.

In the beginning the world was soft and then it quickened and grew firm. Birds were sent down to see if the world were firm enough to hold the animals. They came back and said that the world was still too soft. The great buzzard was sent down from heaven and he flew near to the earth. When his wings touched the soil they beat up mountains and he was recalled to heaven. We were afraid it would all be mountains.

Then the earth became firm and the animals descended onto the earth. The animals lived among the mountains of the earth.

There is a second world within this world. The seasons are different and the light and darkness is different. Our springs and rivers are the same and the sources and the endings of our springs and brooks go and come from the inner world. These springs are the doorways, and to enter the doorways it is necessary to go without food and to be much of the inner world. The seasons of the inner world are different and the heat and cold and light and darkness are different. We know this because in our cold seasons the fresh water from the springs is warm and in the warm seasons it is cold. Within each of us there is also an inner world and within the plants and the animals. There are different seasons when our blood is hot and cold.

When the plants were created we were told to stay awake for seven days and seven nights. We tried, but we fell asleep and so we did not see the creation of the plants. Only the owl and the panther were awake and they were the only ones to see the creation. The plants are also connected with the inner world and within them there is a part of the inner world. Their roots are entrances to the inner world.

The earth is an island set in the middle of a great ocean suspended by four cords from heaven. Heaven is carved from one block of solid rock. When man dries up and the inner world perishes the earth will shrink and the cords will break and the world will go down again into the water. We are afraid of this.

When the myth is over the old man belches and drains the last of his gin out of the bottle. The other Indians talk among themselves and the chief's wife makes coffee in a large white pot and serves it in elegant demitasse cups with gold rims and gilt inscriptions. The chief's wife makes everyone drink two cups of coffee and then she sits down and smokes a borrowed cigarette. She tells Amy all about how the girls go to school and learn to be librarians in the Indian libraries and how lazy the men are and that they do not work.

THE BREAK OCCURS on Thursday afternoon between lunch and dinner. Among the people at the farm there is a young girl who has come down with her mother to spend a week with Amy. She is short and blonde with heavy drooping eyelids, and when she speaks she lifts her face as though to shake back her eyelids and speak up from under her eyes.

It is late afternoon. There are a number of people sitting in the main drawing room smoking and reading. Amy is upstairs working on the typewriter, and the noise comes down into the room like artificial thunder. Suddenly this young girl runs up from the river bank, onto the verandah and into the drawing room. Her hair is shaken loose. Her dress is rumpled. She runs into the drawing room. Her mother is sitting in a chair in the corner. The young girl runs to her and begins to weep convulsively and to beat her head on her mother's breast. She will not talk. They do not know what has happened. Her mother takes her upstairs to the bathroom and washes her face and tries to find out what is the matter.

It was after lunch when it happened. The young girl was walking down by the river. She met the chief on the other side of the bridge. He held her and struggled with her and kissed her. She screamed and beat her fists at him. He took down his trousers and finally she escaped. This is all she can say. Everyone's curiosity is immediately directed to what actually happened. The girl is unable to say. For the rest of the evening she lies on a couch in the drawing room, her face to the wall, sobbing. Amy and her mother consult one another. The young girl is nervous and neurotic and it may be all imagination. While they are in consultation the spokesman of the tribe comes up to the front door bearing under his arm a piece of stove pipe that he borrowed early in the week. He asks for Amy. She crosses the room and meets him at the door again.

—We are leaving tonight, he says.

—Oh, yes. Amy's words are high and empty in the air. She laughs and tells him to put the stove pipe in the barn.

—Business is no good, he says. We are going down to Salbury where there is a roller coaster and a merry-go-round. Here is your money. He hands her a five-dollar bill. She takes it and crumples it up in her jacket pocket.

—Well goodbye, she says. She turns around and comes back into the room. He leaves the stove pipe standing by the front door and returns to the meadow. Within twenty minutes the tents are taken down and the cars go out of the driveway. The meadow is empty. Around the ashes of the camp fire there is a circle of condensed milk tins, candy tinsel, coffee tins, soup tins, paper bags, fruit peelings. The young girl is still in the drawing room, her face to the wall. They tell her that the Indians have gone. They ask her what happened. She answers in a heavy petulant voice.

—In the name of Christ can't you leave me alone. I don't know what happened I tell you, I don't know.

That evening Amy picks up the first impulse of hate and indifference again. They were not real Indians. They were shrewd European gypsies. They had probably picked up the myths and the war dances from books in the public library. There would undoubtedly be a lot of money in the business of becoming primitive Indians for the amusement of civilized Americans. Amy walks back and forth on the verandah looking up at the sticky sweet spring stars. Rachel winds the gramophone, and Amy can hear the thumping of the springs. Then Rachel starts the record. The same record. The repetition is inevitable and pretentious like a miniature doom. The trumpets stem out and flower. The choked shallow voice sings the same explosive words. You can see her standing on the front of the stage. Walking back and forth on the stage shooting out her abrupt smart buttocks.

> Ah need lovin'
> That's what ah crave
> Ah need lovin'
> Ah can't behave

The chorus girls are standing at the footlights. Shaking, vibrating, their hands trembling about their heads.

> Sweet-sixteen-and-never-been-kissed
> Comeon-show-me-what-I've-missed

Amy walks back and forth on the verandah, smelling the soiled spring air, wondering how she is going to pay out the long mornings, the brief evenings of spring and summer. Wondering if lilacs are as fabulous and purple as she remembers. All she can think of is Bock beer and

Bermuda onions.   They will have to clean the meadow out and throw away the tin cans. The river may be high this spring, high enough to flood the vegetable gardens.

Hound and Horn
April-June, 1932

The Autobiography of a Drummer

WAS BORN in Boston in 1869. My family had lived in Boston and had been schoolmasters and shipmasters there ever since anyone could remember. We were poor and my mother was a widow. She ran a boarding house. My other brother and my sister worked and I prepared to go to work as soon as I had finished grammar school. I decided to go into the shoe business and I decided to be a commercial traveler. I wanted to be a commercial traveler as other men want to be doctors and generals and presidents.

When I was twelve years old I left school and got a job as an office boy in a big boot and shoe firm. My salary for the first year was one hundred dollars. Then I was promoted to an entry clerk and my salary for the next year was two hundred dollars. Jobs were not easy to get then and I had to work hard to hold my job. When I went to work the streets were empty and when I came home from work the streets were dark and empty. Finally I got a chance to learn the construction end of the business in a shoe factory in Lynn. I went there and lived in a cheap boarding house and learned how shoes were made. I still know how shoes are made. I can tell the price and sometimes the manufacture of nearly every pair of shoes I see; although sometimes it makes me sick to look at them, they are so cheap. Well, I worked there for five years and in 1891 my salary had grown to seven hundred dollars. That was the year I was given my first chance to sell on the road.

I will never forget that as long as I live. I took a train from Boston to New York and from New York to Baltimore. I like to travel in trains. (Whenever I have spent my vacations in the country I walk down to the depot each day to see the one train come through.) I had a new suit and a new grip and a sample case and a new pair of shoes. The shoes hurt like hell. I've never worn new shoes on a trip since then. My wallet was full of expense money. I like money too. Whenever I have money in my pocket and whenever

I'm taking a train for another city it always seems as though my life were beginning. When I got on that train it seemed as if my life were beginning.

That time I went down to Baltimore, as I have said. I came into Baltimore late one afternoon. I took a sample room at the Carrollton Hotel. There was running water in the room but no bath. The rates were four dollars a day including four big meals if you wanted them. The man who took your hat at the entrance of the dining room, I remember, never gave you a check, but he always returned the right hat to each guest. A ten-cent tip was plenty. The waiters were courteous and distinguished looking. The dining room was on the second floor. I stayed there two days and I made enough to cover my expenses and salary at a little under the estimated selling cost of the home office. When I got back the boss congratulated me.

That was my first success and that was the beginning of a lot of success. My mother had since died and my brother and sister had married. I didn't see much of my mother at the end of her life and I have always regretted this. I didn't have much interest in what my brother and sister were doing. I had my own life. It kept me busy all of the time. Every sign I looked at and every color and shape I saw and even the rain and the snow reminded me of sales talk and shoes. I began to get a reputation. I worked with that firm until 1894 and then I had a better offer out in Syracuse, so I went out there. I was making three thousand dollars a year then. I always traveled by the fastest trains and I had all of my clothes made by a good tailor and I stayed in expensive hotels. I had a lot of friends and a lot of women. The time went quickly. My salary grew larger by a thousand dollars every year.

Those years on the road were the best years and they didn't seem to have any end. I often sold two carloads of shoes over a glass of whiskey. Half of the time I had more money than I knew what to do with. I was successful. I was more successful than I had ever imagined I would be; even when I was twelve years old. I spent all of those years in trains and clubs and hotels. My territory was changed at intervals so that at one time or another I have covered every section of the United States. I know the United States and I love the United States. I can repeat the names of its towns now in hundreds like the names of women and I know the hotels and the timetables and even its train smoke smells sweet to me.

I had ten suits of clothing and twenty pairs of shoes and two sailboats, which I kept in Boston and raced whenever I was in that city. I gambled on the horses at all the big tracks and played Canfield and craps and roulette. I was a Mason and an honorary member of the Elks and I had two large insurance premiums.

My sales record varied as conditions changed, but my income stayed close to ten thousand. It was down on some seasons and way up on others. Droughts, heavy rains, fashions, deaths, scraps between partners, all had their effects on the business but it was fundamentally the same business I had been learning since I was twelve years old. If you lost one customer you could always get another. Buying was done by individuals for individual firms. The shoes I sold were expensive and beautiful. The business also had a seasonal lift because men wore boots in the winter and oxfords in the summer, and nobody ever wore oxfords in the winter. If they did they were crazy.

In 1925 my salary began to decrease, going from ten thousand to eight thousand. I was working for a firm in Rockland then, with my headquarters at the Hotel Statler in Detroit. At the end of that year the firm went out of business. They were beginning to feel the trend in fashion toward inexpensive shoes. They were wise to get out of it when they did and not to hang around like the rest of us suckers.

At the beginning of the next year I went on the road for a firm in Lynn, but they liquidated after I had been with them for nine months. All of the wise men were getting out of the business and forgetting about it. But I couldn't get out of it and I couldn't forget it. I was fifty-seven years old. I was growing old. I couldn't remember anything but trains and hotels and shoes.

After that I tried to find another firm that manufactured the kind of shoes I was used to handling but I couldn't find one. They were all selling out or liquidating. Finally I went on the road selling cheap shoes for a firm in Weymouth, Massachusetts. This was the first time in my life that I had ever sold cheap shoes and I hated to do it.

You had to sell a thousand pairs to make what you could make on a hundred pairs in the old days. My sales hardly covered my commission and salary and expenses. I worked hard and I sold a lot of shoes but I couldn't make any profit. It was like trying to stop it from raining with my two hands. In those last years I never made more than three thousand dollars.

After that all of my trips went in the red. Methods of doing business had changed, faster than I could change. Chain stores and stores owned by manufacturers took the place of stores owned by individuals. Cheap shoes took the place of expensive shoes. Railway fares went up and hotel rates didn't get any lower. The few independent dealers who remained did not buy enough to pay the expenses of selling them. Hand-to-chin buying, we call it. On my sixty-second birthday I was without work. I have not worked since. I am growing old. My insurance policy has lapsed. My money has gone. My brother and my sister are dead. My friends are dead. The world that I know how to walk and talk and earn a living in, has gone. The sound of the traffic below the window of this furnished room reminds me of that.

We have been forgotten. Everything we know is useless. But when I think about the days on the road and about what I have done and what has been done to me, I hardly ever think about it with any bitterness. We have been forgotten like old telephone books and almanacs and gas-lights and those big yellow houses with cornices and cupolas that they used to build. That is all there is to it. Although sometimes I feel as if my life had been a total loss. I feel it in the morning sometimes when I'm shaving. I get sick as if I had eaten something that didn't agree with me and I have to put down the razor and support myself against the wall.

The New Republic
October 23, 1935

In Passing

I WAS LIVING then with Anna and Nicholas Shusser in a house out beyond the race tracks. Nicholas was the manager of a five-and-ten-cent store in the town and I worked for him. I ate all of my meals at the Shussers' and usually spent my evenings with them, sitting in the plot of grass out behind the house, drinking beer. We never did much else. Neither they nor I had the money to go anywhere. But it was nice sitting out in the back yard when we were tired from the store. It was quiet, because most of the houses in the neighborhood were closed. The racing season hadn't begun then.

Anna was beautiful. Nicholas talked all the time. He usually talked about the *lycée* he had attended in Geneva and about their annual *grande course* in the mountains. Then sometimes, after they had gone to bed, I would walk down the road by the race tracks. Preparations were already being made for the season. They were painting and gilding the iron fence that enclosed the tracks and trimming the shrubbery. Some of the horses had arrived, and when you passed down the road you could smell their bodies and the liniments and the manure. A police dog guarded the stables, and whenever I passed down the road he would begin to bark. That end of the town was still empty. The mansions were boarded up. I never met anyone on that road and I never heard anything but the sound of my own heels and the barking of the dog.

Both Anna and Nicholas came from abroad. Anna came from Moscow and Nicholas from Palestine, but his family had moved to Geneva when he was young so that he could get an education at Swiss schools. Although they had been in America for nine years, they still spoke with a strong accent and always talked about Europe. Anna talked about the elevator in her home in Moscow and about the kind of cakes they had for tea. Nicholas talked about the *grande course* or about the way they trapped flies under a glass bell in Palestine. They both loved cities and crowds and they hated that town. But they hated it less than they would hate any other American town, for in some way it resembled the world they were most familiar with: a world of impermanence, travel, train compartments, damp *pensions*, boats. New York stood second to Europe in their minds. They always wanted to go to New York. Anna kept the radio on a New York station all day, and sometimes when we were sitting in the garden drinking beer she would turn her head when she heard the cars passing on the New York highway.

"Those are cars, aren't they, Nick?" she'd say. "Those are cars, aren't they? That noise I hear."

Nicholas would laugh and speak to me. "See Anna, poor Anna. She wants to get out, to get away. Yes, Anna, those are cars going down the New York road."

"How far is New York, Nick?"

"Four hundred miles. Maybe at Christmas you can go down this year."

Anna's mother and sister were in Palestine, and her brother, Lazar, conducted an orchestra in Paris. He was famous and wealthy. They corresponded with one another and she lived for his letters. It seemed strange to her that she should be imprisoned in that little upstate town, with its race track and curative waters and vast, windy hotels, and that she should sit in the back yard and read letters from her brother speaking in terms of thousands of francs earned and spent and thousands of people and crowded, lighted houses.

Nicholas's family were all in America. His brother was a successful chain-store manager in Cleveland and his mother and his sister lived in New York. His sister taught medieval history in a college in the city. He liked his sister; he liked her better than his brother; but he always spoke of her with reserve. Their worlds were different. She was a scholar. She was ugly and absent-minded; he told stories about her absentmindedness. But in the end he would say that he loved her, but she was a scholar and scholars were beyond his understanding.

They had almost no friends in the town. They didn't like the people. Most of the population were dependent upon the racing season, and that fast month of easy money had spoiled them. They had none of the ambition or experience of Anna and Nicholas. They had never been to another town and they never wanted to go to another town, and the faint rush of cars on the highway meant nothing to them. They were malicious and selfish. Nicholas had a few business friends, and sometimes friends of theirs from the city would come up for the races or the cure. Then there were indirect friendships formed through their family. Friends of Nicholas's brother or sister or mother would pass through the town and stop to see them. During the summer months fifty percent of the population of the town was transient. It was the scene of continual arrivals and departures. And so there were always people passing through to see Nicholas and Anna. Girsdansky was one of these.

Neither of them had ever met Girsdansky before. They hadn't even heard the name. I was there when he called up on the phone that night and introduced himself as a friend of Nicholas's sister. Nicholas invited him up to the house. But all that evening before Girsdansky came Nicholas kept trying to remember if at some time he had not heard the name before. All he could think of was a Hebrew scholar with a similar name. He finally decided that Girsdansky would be the scholar. "I'll be glad," he said, "I can talk in Hebrew. It is a better language than Yiddish. Yiddish is nothing. I hope he can stay a long time."

II

GIRSDANSKY CAME UP to the house that night about an hour after he had phoned. We were sitting in the back yard and Nicholas had put a lot of beer on the ice. He was excited. They were both excited, but Anna was quiet. They were excited at meeting a stranger from the city. Finally Girsdansky came. The first thing I heard was his heels on the sidewalk. His step was young and quick. Then I heard his voice in the hallway, while Nicholas greeted him. It was not the voice of a Hebrew scholar. It was the voice of a young man. It was precise and composed and a little flat, like the voice projected by a phonograph. Then he came down into the yard and we all shook hands and Nicholas brought out the beer.

The light in the yard was weak and only a little light came from the kitchen and at first I could hardly see him. At first I thought he was an adolescent. It was his figure and his complexion that gave the impression of an adolescent. His figure was slight and callow, not at all effeminate, but it had none of the development that the figure of a man of his age usually has. It was not gross or thin or crooked or strong. It was the straight callow figure of a boy. And his features had the same unusual youth and simplicity. He was a blond, Polish type. His complexion was as clear and highly colored as a girl's. His hair was brown and wavy and parted in the middle. He wore a pair of steel-rimmed spectacles that flashed in the light from the kitchen when he turned his head. When I first saw him I thought he was seventeen, eighteen years old. He looked like the picture of Sir Galahad that used to hang in the Public Library of the town I come from.

But after we had talked for a little while I knew he was older than that. He was at least in his early thirties. He did not talk like a boy, although his voice had the same clarity and callowness of his figure and his features. He talked like a man. The impression of youth that he gave was largely because he showed no trace of confusion or habit or vice, and because age seems to be indicated by confusion and habit and vice.

We drank a lot of beer and talked, and Nicholas got some crackers and we ate crackers. Girsdansky told Nicholas the news of his sister and his mother and they found they had some common friends in the city and they talked about these. Nicholas told a story about Geneva and the *grande course*. Anna asked Girsdansky if he had ever been to Moscow. Girsdansky said that he was a Communist; he mentioned it casually. He said that he had been sent up there to do some organizing of the Negro workers. He said that he was working for the L—, giving the name of a large organization that was sympathetic to the Communist party. He said that he would be in town for a week and he invited us to two meetings where he was going to speak. Then at about eleven o'clock, he left. He was a little uncertain about finding his way back into town and I wanted to take a walk anyhow, so I offered to walk into town with him.

We walked down the main avenue that led into the town. We talked about Anna and Nicholas and the town. "I've only been here for a couple of days," Girsdansky said, "but the little that I've seen of the town seems to incorporate and intensify all of the corruption and unpleasantness of the capitalist world. These *lumpen* towns are heartbreaking. They will be the last places where the truth is realized. Everywhere you go you see people led on by the delusion of easy money. But even these towns haven't long to go. If you are poor, you eventually have to admit that you are poor. I've talked with a few people and they say that during the last five years the betting goes down and down. There is less business. They tell me that a couple of the gambling houses have closed. Not because of the Federal Government," he said, "but because they can't afford to keep them open. Poverty is a greater force than the Federal Government. Are you a Communist?" he asked.

"No," I said.

"Look at those houses," he said. He pointed to the mansions that lined each side of the street. They were dark and boarded up. "To think of building places like that! It makes me sick. And you find them outside of every small town." He yawned. "I'm tired," he said. "I'm on the go all the time, day and night. I'm with my wife about two months of every year and my son doesn't recognize me. When I leave here I'll have to go down to Pittsburgh and then Philadelphia and then Boston and the mill towns around there. It's a hard job," he said, "but it's worth it."

"How long have you been organizing?" I asked.

"Eight years," he said, "ever since I left college. I studied philosophy," he said. He laughed. "But when I got out I changed my field pretty quick. I've been going up and down the country now for eight years. It's hard work. But there is no work with a greater compensation. I can see how, after eight years, things have changed, and how much nearer we are to a revolution. At first I thought it was something I should never see—or even my son. But now I feel sure I'll see it. And before I'm much older. I hate this world," he said, "and these houses and these streets."

We went down by the dark race track. We could hear our own heels on the road and our own voices. The police dog began to bark. He continued to bark long after we had passed the track and we could hear him barking in the distance. We walked down into the village, down to

the small hotel where he was staying. He explained that the people who owned the hotel had been trying to form a Communist local for some time and that he had been sent up at their request. He said that he was speaking at a Negro church in the South End on the next night. I told him that I'd see him at the meeting. We said good night and I walked back to Shussers' alone.

III

NICHOLAS WAS TOO tired that night to go down to the meeting and Anna stayed home with him. Both Nicholas and Anna liked Girsdansky; but in some way he had disappointed them. "He doesn't smoke," Nicholas said. "He hardly touched his beer. Maybe he didn't like our beer." They had felt somehow that through his clear, temperate, sensible character he was different from them, for Nicholas was confused, intemperate, and extravagant. He loved to spend money, and although they had almost no money, he wasted what they had with great pleasure. He loved extravagance. He used to bring Anna cut flowers when cut flowers were expensive. He felt that extravagance

was a full expression of his character. And it seemed impossible to him that Girsdansky could imagine, in anything but hate and impatience, his love of Anna and money and drink and the world. Girsdansky's slight figure and his young, clear face and his dry voice seemed to show no room for an understanding of those things. In front of Girsdansky, Nicholas felt like a sinner. And so he said he was tired that night and Anna stayed home with him and I went down to the meeting alone.

The meeting was in a little, musty church in the South End. When I came in, the church was nearly full. The audience was half Jewish and half Negro. The Negroes were from the south; they came north every year to work in the stables and at the big hotels. Girsdansky was standing on the platform talking with the preacher. The preacher introduced him. Then Girsdansky began to talk about the Herndon case.

He was careful—very careful. None of the Negroes in the audience had been exposed to Communist propaganda before. They were even suspicious of the term "Communist". But they listened to him while he told the story of An-

gelo Herndon, a young man sentenced for the expression of his opinion, by an ancient, lame law, to certain death on a chain gang. He spoke for about an hour. He was a good speaker; his voice and his presence were attractive and he could lift his voice until it filled the little church. He still looked young and he gave the impression that he would never grow old, since he would never grow old through habit or love or vice. There was a lot of applause at the end of the speech. The Negroes were glad to hear the discrimination they were bitterly familiar with described in terms that implied some rebellion. It was a strange, new world. Then refreshments were served in a vestibule off the church. I stayed to speak with Girsdansky for a minute and then I left.

The night of his second speech was on a Saturday, and Nicholas and I were working late in the store, so neither of us could go. But on Sunday afternoon I met him on Main Street. That was the day before the racing season began and the small street was crowded with traffic and the sidewalk was crowded. I saw him ahead of me long before he saw me. He looked unlike anyone else on the street. He was carrying some books under his arm. He looked as though he didn't see the street or the musty hotels that were being opened then or the touts standing in front of the drugstore. I said hello and we shook hands and I asked him if he wanted a drink. He said that he hadn't eaten his lunch yet, but if I wanted to have a drink while he ate his lunch it would be fine. So we went into a lunch cart near there and he ordered lunch and I ordered a beer.

He looked tired, very tired. He said that he had been working day and night and that he was translating some of the Marx and Engels correspondence in his spare time. "I just got a letter from France today," he said. "My only regrets in this work are that I can't be all over the world at the same time. There's rioting in Havre, Cherbourg, Bordeaux, Calais. That's good news. It brings everything nearer. But the news from Paris isn't so good. That's the Fascist headquarters; I don't have to tell you that, of course. And De la Rocque, financed by the Cotys and the De Wendels, is forming an armed militia of forty thousand men. It's discouraging. Armed men will have to be combated with armed men; and forty thousand is a formidable number to fight against—particularly when our armed militia amounts to exactly one-hundred-and-forty-three men."

He ordered bacon and eggs and drank a couple of glasses of water. He talked and talked and talked. He talked continually about revolution. He talked about history, and about the tendency he saw in that unconscionably long story toward revolution and the dictatorship of the proletariat. He spoke of revolution as if it were something he would see on the next day, or the next, and as if the noise of traffic on Main Street were the noise of military lorries.

"A great deal will depend upon the young men in your generation," he said. "You've had the good fortune to miss the boom period and all of that harmful, inflated ambition. You have never known anything but what it is to be poor. You have probably learned by now," he said, "that there is no greater power than money—inexpressibly greater, to be romantic, than love or death—and that you will never have money in this rotten world and that you will never have power. We depend upon your generation for a great deal, for if anyone has the right to ask revenge or justice it is the young men. And there are twenty million of them," he said, "twenty million men of your age, cooling their heels right now in lunch carts, employment agencies, furnished rooms, buses, or, still worse, in homes, listening to the radio and rereading the paper. Youth is valuable and irretractable. And no man of any courage is going to sit back and take day after day that bears no resemblance to a just and full life. There are twenty million. You know how many that is. Think of it!

"It's simple," he said. "It's as simple as ABC. Anyone who has been poor and helpless and hungry, day after day after day, with no prospects of ever being anything but poor and helpless and hungry, must eventually realize it. It is simple. These are your chains; no iron was ever heavier. And you have to break them. And you can—with your own hands. Can't you realize? Don't you see? It's a new world. No more hunger, no more worrying for tomorrow's food and tomorrow's, no more sitting in a hallway waiting as if you were waiting for a train. It's simple, simple, simple, and everyone, after these years, must come back to justice and reason. It's a rotten world—everyone has had a chance to realize that. Its rottenness pervades everything. The only thing to do is to change it. It is as simple as the desire to eat and drink and live. If a man of any courage or strength finds himself bound hand and foot he will naturally break his bonds. The world is slow to learn, but people will learn. How can they avoid learning? And they are learning! I've seen that during the eight years I've been going up and down the country."

His voice, even when he spoke in hate, was precise and impersonal. He talked like a book; his talk had the clarity and dryness of a book. He ate slowly and uninterestedly. After his eggs he ordered a baked apple and a glass of milk. I kept drinking beer. By that time I knew that he neither drank nor smoked. He had the temperance and the reason and the faith of a saint, and he spoke of another world with the simplicity that a saint would speak of the City of God. "It is simple," he repeated. "It is a matter of pure reason. We are living in a rotten world, shaped by dead hands and ruled by dead hands. We are the young. It is in our power to change it. It is as simple as the desire to eat and sleep and live."

When he had finished eating we went out onto

the street. It was getting dark. The narrow street was crowded. It looked and smelled like a railway depot and it had the feeling of a railway depot. He talked without interruption. ". . . Men are poor. Poverty will define itself to them in these ugly years as an imprisonment worse than any jail. They will realize that there is only one way out. Revolution and the dictatorship of the proletariat—there is not another reasonable answer. There is no other reasonable hope. . . ."

People kept separating us, but he went on talking. He looked different from anyone else on the street. He looked like an American on the streets of London. He was slim and young and he was carrying some books. He did not notice the street or the crowd or the touts or the harlots. He seemed to have less room in his character for a hate of them than he had for plans of what another world would be. "There will be a strike," he said, "this fall. Longshoremen. The docks. The east coast and the west coast. Our marine unions are powerful. . . ."

I walked down to the end of the street with him and then we said goodbye. His work there was finished: the local was organized. He was leaving for Pittsburgh on the following morning. "Goodbye," he said. "Maybe I'll see you in New York. Maybe we'll meet on one of the barricades. It won't be long now." We shook hands. "Goodbye, goodbye."

Then I walked back up the main street, and into the crowd again. I like crowds. The big hotels were open. I went into the bar of the Excelsior and ordered a beer. The season had begun; the bar was full of touts and trainers and horsemen talking about horses. Everywhere there was the tension of a gambling house. Craps and roulette and *chemin de fer* tables were set up in a casino in the courtyard. I went down and watched the gaming for a little while and the faces above the tables. They were intent and greedy. The players were not rich. The betting was low, and some of the people, particularly some of the women, were shabbily dressed: but there was nothing in their faces but a love of money and the incorrigible dream of big money. Dance music was coming from the dining room, and from the street beyond the hotel I could hear the noise of traffic, the noise of cars from every state in the Union, crowding into the village for the races, like the crippled pilgrims at the news of another miracle in Lourdes or Seville or Sainte-Anne-de-Beaupré.

IV

THE RACING SEASON lasted five weeks and I stayed there until the end of the meet. Like the rest of the town, I bought dope and played the races, and on the last day Nicholas gave me the afternoon off and I went down and saw Corabelle win the Hopeful. She wasn't the favorite; she had a bad post position, and she didn't take the lead until halfway through the race, but then she nosed her way down the crowd, sweeter and faster than anything in the world with that faint thunder of hoofs, stirring you like something you remember but can't place; and everyone went wild, yelling and screaming and throwing up their programs. And that night we could hear, from the back yard at Shussers', the horse vans going down the southern highway to Aqueduct and Belmont Park, as if they were dragging the breath out of that village, leaving a settlement of musty, empty rooms.

When the season ended, there wasn't much

business in the store. I planned to go back to Manhattan. I planned to go back there until I received that letter from my father. "I feel that you ought to know," he wrote, "that we are leaving this house after thirty years. The bank has fore-closed the mortgage and sold the land to Standard Oil. They are going to tear down the house and put up a gas station here. We are going to take an apartment in Adams. Jim is going to boarding school, although I don't know where the money is going to come from. I don't know what is going to happen to the rugs and furniture, etc. . . . I don't know what your mother's plans are yet. But we should like to see you before we leave here and if you could come down we should be very grate-ful." And so a few days later I said goodbye to Anna and Nicholas. They went down to the bus depot with me. We shook hands.

"Goodbye, stranger."

"Goodbye, Anna, Nick."

"If you could only have had better weather," Anna said. "It makes me lonely. Cold, rainy. I hope it isn't cold on the bus."

"Goodbye, stranger," Nicholas kept saying. Then the bus started up and we went down the long

road an d out of the Adirondacks. It was good to
be on the road again. It was rainy and cold. Some
of the grass along the road had begun to take on
color and some of the swamp maples had turned
and the mountains all around the sky were purple.
Most of the roadside stands had closed and it
looked like autumn. We came into Albany late that
night. It was still raining—a light, cold rain. I
walked around the streets and spent the night in
the bus depot. In the early morning I took a bus to
Boston. That trip took nearly all day. We went
through the flat, cultivated valley of the Connecti-
cut and crossed Lebanon Mountain and left the
Berkshires for the straight turnpikes of my own
country and that worn landscape with its hotels
and roadhouses and gas stations. We came into
Boston a little before dark. I took an evening train
to the cape where our home was. My father met
me at the depot. I had written them the day I was
coming and so he was there when I got off the train.

He looked a little older. He was in his early
sixties then, and had not worked for a long time.
He was living off a little royalty money he received
for an invention he had designed some time before.
He had made a lot of money in his life and had

spent a lot of money. He loved to spend money; extravagance seemed to be the fullest expression of his character, and when he lost this power he grew old quickly. He looked older than his age that evening when he met me. But I was very glad to see him.

I drove the car down to the house that night, and when we came down on to the highway I could see it ahead of me. It was a large, rambling house, which had been built before the Revolution. It was the house that I had been born in and that my parents expected to die in. The rooms were lighted, and when we came up the drive my brother and my mother came out to meet me. It was good to be back. It was better than I could have imagined. Nearly everything was unchanged. My brother was taller and stronger; he was seventeen years old then, five years younger than I. My mother didn't seem to have changed any. Her hair was gray. She was wearing a fresh linen dress. She looked a little tired, but she looked the same.

I had a couple of drinks and some supper in the kitchen. My brother wanted to know about the races and I told him about Corabelle. "I'd like to go up there next season," he said. "I've never seen a real race. I'd like them, I guess. I'd have good luck with my bets; I usually have good luck. I got two dollars out of the jackpot down at the corner last week." I told them everything I could remember and then I walked through the house with my mother. Neither of us mentioned the fact, that night, that they were leaving the house. She took me through the rooms as if she enjoyed it as much as I did and as if it would be hers forever. "See," she said, "everything's the same, isn't it?" Everything was the same. There were the same Turkey carpets and portraits of my grandmother and my brother and myself, and the handsome, shabby furniture and curtains and books and the cast of Venus de Milo. She took me through all of the rooms. "Your room is just the same," she said, "isn't it? Jim wanted to take down the snowshoes, but I wouldn't let him. He has a pair of his own. And whenever he takes out the books I make him put them back where he found them. The moths got into that carpet. I guess it's because you weren't around to spill your cigarette ashes. But we had it mended. You wouldn't know the difference, would you?" Then we went back to the kitchen.

We were all happy and we were all talking at once. "I found your steam engine up in the attic," my brother said. "You know—the electric one. I've got it now so it can cut wood. And I took apart the old rheostat and fixed it so I can candle the lights in my room. I'm going to take it back to school with me."

"Did you get any long shots?" my father asked. "I read in the paper that a sixty-to-one horse came in. I wondered if you had any money on her. I thought about you when I read it."

"Would you like something more to eat?" my mother said. "I made some Chess cakes yesterday and there's an Edam in the ice chest." Finally we all went upstairs. I was tired. I talked with my brother for a little while in the hallway. He told me his plans for returning to boarding school and about the college he wanted to go to and about the basketball team. Then I undressed and went to bed.

V

I SPENT THE FIRST couple of days cutting wood. The woodbins were empty and my parents didn't want to order another cord because they were moving so soon and because they had a long bill at the wood dealer's. They had bills everywhere. And so I felled a couple of trees and cut them into lengths with my brother and split them for the fireplaces. There wasn't much else to do. We inflated the old football and passed it back and forth in the yard. I went swimming in the lake a couple of times and in the afternoons I walked out into the woods behind the barn that stretched to the south for thirty miles without a house or a road. And in the evenings I sat in the kitchen and read *The Conquest of Mexico*.

Neither of my parents seemed bitter or greatly disturbed over the fact that they were being forced to leave the house. They only spoke of it when they were reminded of some preparation that would have to be made. So far they had done nothing. My mother wanted everything left as it was until the day the moving men came. And they didn't seem greatly disturbed over the fact that they were poor. My father still smoked cigars and my mother still went through the grocery store, trailed by a couple of clerks, buying anything she wanted. They owed money everywhere. They had lost their credit, but they lived comfortably, day after day, with the little cash they had. They didn't know what they were going to pay the rent of their apartment with when they moved or who was going to pay Jim's board and tuition at school. I worried about it. Finally I asked my mother. "Don't worry," she said. "We haven't any money, that's true. But we've always been able to find some. And I guess our luck won't break now. The lame and the lazy are provided for. Remember the lilies of the field. . . ."

I decided then to go on to New York. There was nothing much I could do there. I decided late one afternoon when I had gone swimming alone and when I was walking back from the lake. The water had been cold and the air was cold. It was a cold, gray day. It looked like rain and some jays in the orchard were calling for rain. Then I noticed the two men in the orchard behind the house. They had on riding breeches and high, laced boots. They had surveying instruments and they were surveying the level of the ground where the house was. I knew they were from the oil company. I didn't say anything to them. I walked through the orchard up to the house.

My mother was in the cookroom cutting out biscuits with the bowl of a wineglass. "Tom," she said, when I came into the room, "who are those men out there? They've been there most of the afternoon. Do you know who they are?"

"No," I said, "I don't know who they are. I guess they're surveyors from the oil company."

"Don't they know we're still living here?" she said. "I wish they wouldn't do anything until we go. I asked them at the bank and they promised they wouldn't. We're going soon enough. I wish you'd ask them to leave," she said. "Tell them to come back the first of the month. We'll be gone then. Tell them this is still private property."

"Sure," I said.

I went out and told them they were trespassing on private property and that this would remain private property until the first of the month. They thought I was fooling, so I told them again. Finally they packed up their stuff and went off. I went back to the kitchen. My mother was still cutting out biscuits. She didn't say anything about the surveyors.

"Tell me about the races," she said, "Or about the place where you worked or the people you stayed with. You haven't told me anything yet.

I've never been up there. I always wanted to go when I was young, but we never made it. Tell me about the town. Does it look anything like the pictures on the bottle labels? That's the only idea I have of it. The pictures on the Vichy bottles."

She suddenly turned pale. She had pressed too hard on the wineglass and the base had broken and the stem had stuck up into her palm. The blood spurted over the table. "I've cut myself," she said. "I guess I've cut myself." She sank into a chair beside the table. The blood was running all over her fingers and dripping onto the floor. I staunched the cut with a napkin and got some cold water. She told me where the iodine and the bandages were. When I came back into the room she was whiter than her linen dress. I swabbed the cut with iodine and clumsily wrapped a bandage around her palm. "That's all right," she said. "It's not such a bad cut. I was lucky, I guess. It might have been much worse. It's not such a bad cut. We're always lucky," she said bitterly. She began to cry. She cried like a young girl. She gasped for breath as if she were suffocating.

"Why do they have to come while we're still here?" she said. "Why can't they wait until we go?

— 73 —

We're going. We'll be gone in a little while. Why can't they wait? Oh, I can't stand it!" she cried. "I can't stand it any longer. It's too much to ask of anyone. This is our house; my sons were born here; I want to die here. For thirty years we've been working, saving, trying to find something, anything. And now it's all gone. We're poor. We have to count each penny. I lie in bed at night worrying about the bills. I can't sleep. We haven't anything, Tom," she cried. "We haven't anything, anything! Do you know what this is? You can't know; you're too young. We haven't a place to rest in, a place to die in. We may die in a hotel. On the street. We haven't anything, Tom, anything! Oh, sit down beside me," she said. "Give me a cigarette.

"I'm tired," she said. "I guess I'm tired out." She had been crying for a long time then. She stopped. She was speaking in a low voice, nearly as if she were speaking to herself. "I wouldn't mind it so much," she said, "if I were younger or older. I wouldn't mind it if I were an old woman. If there wasn't this horrible fear all the time! We're poor sinners, I guess, and everything we own and everything we know and love and remember is open to dust and rust. But it doesn't seem right that we should lose everything, after all these years, everything! It seems to be against everything I have ever known or ever expected to know. It seems as if we ought to be able to make a decent living."

It was growing dark in the kitchen. The last gray light was going out of the windows. I heard my father coming down the stairs.

"Don't mention this to your father," she said. "Don't say anything about this to him, will you? Make the tea for me—all you have to do is pour some hot water into the pot. There's some cake in the cakebox. Put it on a fresh plate."

There was a fire in the living room and I took the tea in there. "Don't mention this to your father," she said, "will you?" She sat down by the fire and tasted her tea and watched the fire. "There isn't much sense in crying, I guess. But sometimes it gets me down. And I don't suppose we have much to cry about. We have plenty to eat; our clothes are whole. And we'll get some money, somehow. We always have, we always will." She spoke dryly, then. She spoke without any trace of having cried. "We're lucky. I mean it. We'll find some money somewhere. It's always like this. We get down to the bottom, then something comes along. We'll find some money— lots of it. Maybe I can borrow some from the bank. They ought to loan us a few dollars. That would be a start. That would tide us over until something else turns up."

My father came into the room and sat down.

"You know," she said to him, "we might be able to borrow some money from the bank. We've been good customers of theirs. I know Mr Godfrey. He's influential there. He might be willing to help. We might be able to borrow a few hundred dollars."

"Sure," my father said, "sure. I don't see why we can't borrow money from the bank. We've been good customers of theirs for thirty years. That's what the money's there for—to be borrowed."

"Not much," she said, "but a few hundred. Enough to tide us over."

"It seems funny to talk about money the way we talk about money now," he said. "It seems funny, doesn't it? It wasn't like that in the old times, Tom, let me tell you. Why, you know I was working for Flint. I worked for him for a few years and then I had a better offer out in Syracuse, so I resigned. So when I resigned Flint calls me into his office and gives me a drink and asks me if they owe me any money. 'No,' I says, 'no, I don't think you owe me any money.' Well, he rings for his secretary and says, 'Make Mr Morgan out a check for a couple of thousand.' Just like that. Just like that he gave me a couple of thousand. Why, I used to go over to New York once a month, and Flint used to come along with me—just to have a good time, you know. We used to get the five o'clock train, get into New York about ten, and start hitting it up then.

"Well, one night we were going over on that train and before dinner we went up to the smoker for a couple of drinks. While we were in the smoker I see Danny Donnelly. He and I used to go to grammar school together and we boxed in the same gymnasium. Well, he had been playing bull on the market then and he was a millionaire. I went over and spoke to him and when I came back Flint asked me who my friend was. I told him and he asked me to have him eat dinner with us. It was agreeable to Donnelly, so we all went up to the diner together. All the time Donnelly thought Flint's name was Flynn. He thought he was another Irishman. See? So when we sit down the first thing he does is to order a bottle of Gold Seal. Then I order a bottle of Gold Seal. Then Flint orders a bottle of Gold Seal."

He broke out laughing. He laughed so that it was hard for him to speak. "Well, we drank every quart of champagne they had on that train," he said. "Then we had to start ordering pints. Honestly! We drank every quart. We stayed in that car until the train came into Grand Central about ten o'clock. Oh, those were the days, those were the days!"

His voice was kind and genial. He spoke as if he were conscious of the warm room and the cold evening. "We had plenty of money then," he said, "plenty of money. But we'll have it again— don't you worry." He was speaking to my mother then. He was speaking to her with the confidence and ease of their love that, after thirty years, had left them as indulgent of one another and as hopeful as a young man and a girl. "We'll have it again. Maybe our horse will come in on the sweepstakes. I have a sweepstakes ticket. If we could win one of those prizes we wouldn't have to worry about money again. It's a good ticket. A friend of mine, a Canadian, sold it to me. We might win, you know. I wouldn't be surprised. I found some four-leaf clovers out behind the barn. The frost had killed everything but them. They're the first four-leaf clovers I've found this year. That means good luck."

My brother came into the room. He poured himself a cup of tea and sat down.

"Why do we always have tea?" he said. "Why do we always drink tea?"

"Because I'm English," my mother said, "and because English people drink tea. If you don't like tea you can make yourself some coffee."

"No," he said, "I don't want coffee. I just wondered why we always drank tea."

"Or I might get some more money on my patent," my father said. "They might increase the royalty. Lots of men make ten, twelve thousand dollars a year on a patent."

My brother got up and crossed the room. There was an old steel engraving of Egypt on the wall.

"Have any of you people ever been to Egypt?" he asked.

"I've never been to Egypt," I said.

"Alexandria, Karnak, Cairo," he said. "The names sound nice. I'd like to go there. I will go there some day."

"Where do you think you'll live in New York?" my mother said.

"I don't know," I said. "Somewhere on the West Side."

"Listen to that wind," she said. "It sounds like winter. There'll be big waves on the lake tonight. It'll be cold out there."

"Did you know that this knife was made in France?" my brother asked. He had picked the knife off the cake plate and was examining the blade. *"Fait en France*, it says, *M Pouzet. Médaille d'or. Exposition 1878. Lyon.* Lyons. That's a city in France, isn't it? I'll go there some day. Lyons, Marseilles, Paris—all those cities." He lifted the knife up so that my mother could see it. "Did you know it was made in France?" he said.

VI

I PLANNED TO take the night train from Boston.

My brother drove me into the city on the day I left. It was raining. There was a light, high wind from the coast, beating the smoke down onto the roofs. The wind and the rain were cold. I said goodbye to my parents. My brother raced the car down the drive. The road was empty and straight and wet, and he drove the car as fast as it would go.

"Have you ever seen a Dusenberg?" he asked.

"Yes," I said. "I've seen and driven a Dusenberg."

"Gee," he said, "I'd like to drive one. I'd like to drive a Lancia—a real racing car. Or an airplane. I'd like to get a pilot's license. But it takes a lot of money to get a license unless you're in the army. Maybe if there's a war I'll volunteer as an aviator. Then I'll get all the flying I want for nothing. But I hope there isn't a war. It'll spoil my plans. You can't do much while there's a war going on. And there are lots of places I want to go and things I want to do."

"I'm going to Technology," he said. "I want to take up engineering. I don't want to stop at that, of course, but it will be a good beginning. I can make some money and I can travel. I want to make a lot of money, and I want to travel. I don't think I'll get married right off. I'll wait a little while longer. I'd like to look around and spend money on women. If you have money you can know all kinds of women."

"I've been reading some of the books in your room," he said. "I don't read much, but I like some of those books. The lives of the generals— Hannibal, Alexander, Caesar.

"How is it in New York?" he asked.

"Oh, it's all right," I said. There wasn't much else I could say. I couldn't tell him about sitting in a furnished room day after day, living on chocolate and stale bread.

"I want to make a lot of money," he said. "I like money and I like women and I like to travel and go fast. I'm going to do all of that before I settle down."

When we came into the city it was getting dark. It was still raining. I said goodbye to my brother. I checked my valise and bought my ticket and walked uptown. It was cold—like winter. The wind was blowing the leaves off the trees on the Common. The sidewalk was covered with wet leaves.

I walked down to the mall. There was a political speaker on the south side of the walk. Only a handful of people were listening to him. But he was addressing the trees and the wind and the sky as if he were addressing thousands. It was Girsdansky. I recognized him from a distance by his spectacles and his dry, slightly rasping voice. "It is simple," he was saying. "It is a matter of pure reason. We are living in a rotten world, shaped by dead hands and ruled by dead hands." He was speaking with the same intensity and purity that he had spoken to me on the streets of the spa.

"It is in our power to change it. There is only one way out—the dictatorship of the proletariat. It is as simple as the desire to eat and sleep and live. . . ."

I didn't stay there long; it was too cold to stand still. I didn't speak to him. I don't know whether he recognized me or not. I walked down Charles Street scuffing up the dead leaves and wondering where I should be in that season in another year.

The Atlantic Monthly
March, 1936

Bayonne

THE LUNCH CART was in the market district near the shore of the North River. The sidewalk was lined with boxed vegetables and fruits and the chicken market, smelling of warm mould and manure, was only a block away. The street always seemed to be jammed with trucks and wagons. The Ninth Avenue "el" ran overhead and you could hardly hear the noise it made above the roar of the traffic and the shouting and baying claxons on the interstate trucks. Most of the customers were market-men or trucksters. There wasn't much business in the late morning. A few men came in for buns and coffee, that was all. But at noon the place was so crowded that you had to wait ten minutes sometimes for a stool to sit on. Then at half-past one business would begin to get slow and at half-past two the place would be empty again, excepting a few men drinking coffee or hanging around the baseball machine. The district emptied in the same way and at seven o'clock the neighborhood was silent and deserted excepting some men, standing on the piers, watching the harbor traffic or an empty cross-town trolley car or a drunk, stumbling along the sidewalk, heading for the saloons further north. At seven o'clock they mopped up the lunch cart, stacked the chairs onto the tables and closed the place until morning.

The crowded noon hour was the only thing that kept the place going. There were four men working the counter and then on the other side of the cart there was a single line of tables and they had a waitress to serve these. Her name was Harriet but everyone called her Bayonne. One day one of the butchers had asked her where she came from.

"Bayonne," she said.

"I do too," he said.

"Quit your kidding," she said.

"I'm not kidding, that's straight."

"Hey, Bayonne," one of the other men at the table shouted, "draw one." She answered him and after that everyone called her Bayonne.

She was a woman in her early forties and she had

been married once but she was living alone then.

"What street do you live on?" one of the men asked her.

"Macon Street."

"Live with your family?"

"No, I live alone."

"Married?"

"Used to be."

"Hey Bayonne, service."

She never had much time to answer their questions fully but she always gave them some reply as she raced between the tables and the serving counter with the loaded trays. She wore a black uniform and a pair of low-heeled, dusty shoes that were cracked and run to the sides with use. Her face was full and pleasant and her nose was slightly crooked as if it had been broken. Her hair was dyed a lustreless straw-color but the original shade, a much deeper blonde, showed at the parting in the middle of her head. It was curled in brief, unnatural waves that looked as though they had been set with a scorching iron. Her figure wasn't good. Her calves were thick and heavy and her breasts were flat. She carried herself well. She walked as if she were beautiful and attractive and

as if she knew it. While she was waiting for orders she would give a reassuring touch to the hair at the back of her head and smile at the men sitting by the counter. All of them liked her.

The only time that she was really rushed was during the two hours at noon, but it was hard and steady work then. The tables held about fifty people and she had to wait on all of them. They shouted their orders and she repeated them to the counter-man who bawled them out to the men at the steam-tables. Along with this she tried to keep up a conversation and flirt with the customers. The rush made her hoarse and killed her legs, but she liked it. She liked it so much that in the mornings before it began, she was restless. She would walk back and forth before the empty windows, patting the hair at the back of her head, looking out of the dingy windows at the traffic. She would take a small compact out of the pocket of her uniform and powder her nose in the mirror above the cigarette machine. She would cross the cart and lean on the counter and watch the men load the steam-tables.

"I wish they'd hurry up and come in. I'd rather work than hang around like this."

"They'll be plenty to do, Bayonne. What's your hurry?"

"Oh, I don't know. But I'd rather work than hang around like this."

At about noon the men would begin to crowd in. All of them said hello to her and she smiled and answered all of them. She was not pretty but she was attractive in the way she answered their questions and reached across their shoulders and in the way she carried herself. Gradually the din in the place would increase. The conversation of the customers would rise to a roar above the clatter of dishes and the bawling counter-man and her loud, clear voice.

"Hey, Bayonne."

"Over here, Bayonne."

"Some pie, Bayonne."

She raced back and forth, laughing and joking and holding hands with the customers while they decided on their orders. The din and the admiration of the men and the rattle of crockery seemed to intoxicate her like the swelling rain of applause to an actress or the thunder of hooves and the smell of tan-bark to a racing tout. Her step was light and firm and quick and although the place was crowded, she always worked her way quickly through the crowd and never dropped or spilled the dishes. She walked with her head up, occasionally shaking it to toss back the dry, straw-colored hair. Her body then was unconsciously alive and vital, her eyes were bright and she smiled continually, the quiet, restrained smile of a woman walking in the power of men's admiration. But at half-past two it was all over. She was tired then. She would mop off the tables and go into the washroom for a cigarette and talk with the chef through the open door.

"Tired, Bayonne?"

"Yeah. But I like it. You know you get to like it."

She had been working there for two years, doing all of the work without any help, when the uptown management decided to send her an assistant. That was the way the management usually worked. The head counter-man received the notice and he told her about it.

"You're going to get an assistant, Bayonne," he said.

She was standing at the other end of the cart, looking out of the window.

"What's that?"

"You're going to get an assistant."

She walked down the cart.

"You mean I'm going to have someone to help me wait on the tables."

"That's it."

"But I don't need any help."

"I know you don't. But you can't do anything about it. If they want to throw away another salary it's all right by me."

"They must be crazy," she said.

"They are, but it's not our fault."

"Is it going to be a woman?"

"I guess so."

"When's she coming?"

"This morning."

Bayonne sighed and sat down on one of the stools. "I'd rather do it alone," she said, "It's going to make a lot of trouble. She'll be dumb and I'll have to break her in. It was going all right. Why do they have to butt in? They don't know anything about it. We'll be stepping all over each other." That was all she saw in it then. She could take care of the customers herself and it irritated her to think of dividing the work and breaking in another girl. But at ten o'clock, when the girl came in, looking around confusedly and wondering if she had the wrong address, Bayonne knew that it would mean something else. She went into the washroom and looked at herself in the mirror.

The other girl was much younger. She was about twenty. She had worked in lunch carts before and she knew how to do the work. She had the manners of an old waitress, restrained, flirtatious and cynical. Her posture was erect and easy, as erect as a singer's. Her legs were trim and her figure was good. When a man asked her for the ketchup she smiled and said quietly, "There isn't anything I wouldn't do for you." Her arms, reaching across the counter for orders, were slim and white compared to Bayonne's scrawny, muscular arms.

Bayonne didn't have to teach her anything. She was perfect. When the rush began she took half of the tables and waited on them smoothly and quickly. Bayonne kept watching her, not because she was afraid she would make some mistake, but in order to see whether the men she had served for so long would miss her or be satisfied with the younger substitute. The men didn't seem to miss her at all. She looked anxiously for the faces that were the most familiar and attractive and saw them happily kidding the other girl. She was so distracted during the first of the rush that she kept bringing the wrong orders and slopping coffee into the saucers. Then she decided to forget about it and put all of her attention into the work. But the men kept reminding her.

"Got some competition now, Bayonne?"

"Is she your daughter?"

"Who's the new girl?"

At two o'clock the business fell off and they began to get the tables cleared and the dishes washed. At three the place was nearly empty. Bayonne went over to the other girl and asked her how she liked it.

"Oh, it's all right," she said. "I've seen worse. I like it all right."

"It's a good business," Bayonne said, "but it wears you down. Look at my legs." She shrugged her shoulders. "And I use to have good legs too."

"It does wear you down," the girl said, "but I'm used to it. I've been doing it for a couple of years now." She spoke with dry, indifferent acceptance.

"Where did you work before?"

"Up in Yorkville. It was all right. About the

same size as this place only the business was slower and steadier."

"If it was slower and steadier here it would be easier to take care of. It's the two hours rush and then sitting around for the rest of the time that takes it out of you."

At five o'clock she changed from her uniform into street clothing. When she had finished dressing she waited for the younger girl.

"Want to go out for a beer?" she said.

"Sure. I've got a date at six but I guess I've got the time."

They went into the back room of a saloon around the corner. Bayonne ordered two lagers.

"I don't drink much," she said, "and I don't like beer, but what else can you drink on the salary we get? And if I drink too much I can't work well on the next day and that job takes everything."

"How long have you been here?"

"Two years."

"How's the management?"

"Awful. Honestly. They'll fire you without notice or transfer you to another cart. They're the worst company I ever worked for."

The young girl tasted her lager. She didn't say

anything.

"You're pretty young to get into this, aren't you?" Bayonne said.

"Oh, I don't know. I'm young enough, I guess, but I can't seem to find anything else to do."

"I shouldn't think you'd have much trouble in finding something to do. You're young and good-looking. I should think you'd get a job in a class restaurant uptown somewheres. Have you ever tried?"

"I've tried but I've never had the money to register at any of the good agencies."

"How much does it cost?"

"Fifteen or twenty dollars."

"I'll lend you the money."

The girl looked at her curiously. "You mean you'll lend me the money to register?"

"Sure. That's it."

"But why should you want to loan me money to get a job? I don't understand you. If you've got the money why don't you try it yourself? And you don't know me anyhow. You've never seen me before. I might never show up again."

"Oh, I know you're all right. I can see it in your face. And I just don't like to see a young girl like you wasting yourself in a place like that."

"But I don't mind it."

"No. You don't mind it now, but you will. It gets you down. It spoils your legs and your health. You're too tired to go out at night. Sometimes I'm so tired I can't even sleep."

"Listen," the girl said, half standing, "it's twenty minutes of six and I've got to get uptown. I'll see you in the morning."

"Wait a minute, wait a minute, let's get this straight. If you want to sign off this job, I'll bring the money tomorrow morning and you can apply at one of the agencies. I'm just doing it for your own good. I don't want to see you wasting your life in that place."

"But why should you get so worried about me? I'm all right. And you don't know me anyhow. I don't understand you."

She looked at the younger girl steadily and curiously as if she were looking at herself in a mirror. "No, I guess you can't understand me," she said quietly. "I guess you're too young to understand me. I guess you've never known what it feels like. And I can't think of anything that would make you understand. Have you ever fallen asleep with your clothes on and felt cold and stiff when you woke up and found out that it had grown dark? Have you ever? It's something like that. And then. . ."

"Listen," the younger girl said, "I've got to get uptown. I'll be late. I'll see you in the morning."

She stood and fished in her purse for a dime and put it down on the table.

"That's for the beer," she said. "I'll see you in the morning."

"Wait a minute, wait a minute."

"I'll see you in the morning," she repeated. She was still trying to be polite. "Goodbye," she said. She walked through the bar-room and out the door.

Bayonne heard the door close. She drained her glass and gathered her purse and gloves and looked at herself in the mirror. Then she paid for the beer and went out onto the street. She glanced up at the sky. It was whitening. The neighborhood was already empty. She walked south along the deserted sidewalk.

She didn't turn up for work on the next morning or on any of the mornings that followed; she didn't even come back for her clothing that still hangs there from a hook in the washroom.

Parade
Spring, 1936

The Princess

SHE WAS JUST an ordinary girl in the line until Golden got hold of her. She was younger than most of them; she must have been about twenty. She had a lot of energy and she was really interested in the work. She had been to a big dancing school in New York for a couple of years and she could do back-bends and high kicks and toe-dancing and in the finale, when the girls came, one by one, down the staircase, she did a high-kick number at the front of the stage, but that was just to make the finale look legal and no one ever looked at her and it was like talking to the backs of a crowd. She wasn't a princess of course. It wasn't even her idea. Golden thought it up. He even thought up the name for her. He billed her as the glamor-ous Princess Nika from South America. Her real name was Dorothy. She wasn't glamorous and she didn't know anything about South America except that it was the place where some of those rusty freighters, shored off Brooklyn, came from.

It was in her second year on the stage when the show was rehearsing in New York for the road, that Golden began to push her. She was his girl then and he was probably the first man she had ever known. He did it more out of kindness than anything else. She didn't have the make-up to be a good teaser or even a dancer. Her face was pretty and stupid. You could nearly count her breast-bones and her breasts were flat. The muscles on her legs were overdeveloped and she walked with a slight spring. She never talked about her family or about the town she came from, but you could tell she came from the west, even if she had picked up a strong New York accent, and it would be one of those tank-towns you see in the evening from the windows of the bus with a light burning in the drugstore. She was ambitious. Her parents had spent nearly all of their money to send her through dancing school and her obligation to them and her memory of them as they would be waiting then, for the news of her success, was one of the reasons why she was so ambitious. She wanted to be famous and successful. She wanted it more than she would ever want any man.

It may have been through understanding this that Golden put her ahead. He took her out of the line and filled the lobby in Brooklyn with her pictures and gave her bigger billings than anyone else. She had four legitimate dances, two before and two after the intermission. She led the chorus and she had the stage to herself for the best part of five minutes. She had worked up the dances herself and drilled the chorus and picked her own scenery out of the warehouse. Of course she wasn't important to the show. They just kept her on because Golden liked her and because it made the thing look legitimate.

The sudden promotion didn't make her vain or overbearing. It only made her more serious and heightened her preoccupation with work and success. She worked the girls hard, but she was careful not to overwork them. She worked herself, day and night. She used to beg the pianist to stay around after the rehearsal was over so that she could go through her entrances again. Golden would come into the theatre after midnight and find her there alone, humming the music to herself and prancing up and down in front of an imaginary line of girls.

When they went on the road Golden went with them as far as Philadelphia. They made some changes in the show there and he let her introduce a new dance number. It was a fast number and she worked hard for it, but somehow it didn't get over. In the finale the orchestra broke, passing the melody to a solo trombone; she pushed her hat over onto her forehead and strutted off into the wings, pumping her walking stick like a baton. It was all right. She did it all right. But somehow it was stale as if you knew how she had rehearsed the number in front of a looking-glass night after night after night.

Golden left the show then and went back to New York, leaving Bacon, the straight man, in charge. Bacon went right on giving her the best billings and running her four specialities. He did it more out of habit than anything else. No one thought much about her. No one saw much of her off the stage. She always took a furnished room by herself when they stayed in a town and she never talked much in the dressing room. Sometimes she ate supper with the company after the show. She didn't smoke because she was afraid it would spoil her wind for dancing. She didn't drink either. For supper she usually ate a salad without dressing and a slice of bread. The only qualities that distinguished a member of the company for the girls were drink and overbearing vanity, and as she was sober and quiet they nearly forgot about her. But one night she surprised them. They were eating supper in a cafeteria in Baltimore. Bacon came into the cafeteria with the man who owned the hotel they were staying in. He introduced him to the girls. Dorothy was sitting at a crowded table with her back to the wall.

". . . and this is Dorothy," Bacon said. "Mr Brody."

She looked up and smiled at him.

"My name isn't Dorothy," she said, "and you know it. I'm Princess Nika."

"Well, Dorothy to us," Bacon said.

She glanced up at him again. Her smile was cool and dirty.

"Princess Nika to you," she said, "and to everybody else."

"All right," he said, "all right. Princess Nika;

Mr Brody."

She seemed satisfied then. She seemed to have found some deep satisfaction. You could see that she wasn't fooling. Bacon had thought she was fooling at first because she had replied to him in the cool, undoubting voice that only a faith-less remark or a deep belief is made in and it never occurred to him that she would believe in what she was asking. But then he saw, a second later, that she did believe. He felt as if he had been talking sympathetically to a person who turns out suddenly to be insane.

From Baltimore they went over to Pittsburgh. They took the bus at night and came into the depot at Pittsburgh a little after dawn. It was a cool morning and the company stood on the side-walk outside the depot while the porter unloaded the luggage. The streets were empty and there was nothing to look at but the low row of build-ings across the street and a sprinkler truck coming slowly down the street, wetting the pavement. The girls stood there watching the porter hand down the luggage from the roof of the bus. The first girl who noticed it broke out laughing. She was tired and it seemed funny. Then she pointed it out to one of the other girls. Printed at the end of Dorothy's trunk were the initials "H.R.H. Nika." It looked as if she had printed them there herself. It was done in yellow paint and the letters were shaky.

These discoveries and changes were stronger as reflections in the company's opinion of her than any changes in the way she acted herself. The girls joked about her in the dressing-room but she didn't seem to mind. She had a quiet self-confidence that could stand anything. She was as quiet in the dressing-room as she had always been and she still worked very hard. She had made a few changes in her dances and she was working by herself in a new tap number. She was planning to do a solo tap-dance to the overture of *Il Trovatore*. She rehearsed it for a couple of weeks and then Bacon let her put it on. The orchestra wasn't very good on the music and she went so fast that the line couldn't follow her. She worked hard. She worked harder than any of the girls had ever seen anyone work. But when she came off there was just a splatter of applause and Bacon told her, later that night, that he thought she'd better drop the number.

"I'm not going to drop it," she said quickly, "and you can't make me."

He was surprised to see her get so excited.

"And if you think you're going to make me drop it," she said, "I'll wire Golden and he'll tell you where you stand."

He didn't know whether she ever wired Golden or not. She never said anything more about it and he finally forced her to drop the number. He figured that she must have wired Golden and that he hadn't answered. He wouldn't answer. He would have forgotten all about her by then. Bacon knew that. And he felt that a shakedown would be good for her.

They hit Chicago in a hot spell and business was bad. Bacon had expected it all along. There was hardly enough business to keep them going and he decided to make the show faster and dirtier to see if that would build up an audience. He did it without any serious desire to hurt Dorothy or at least he didn't fully realize a desire to hurt her. Her numbers weren't any good. She'd have to learn that some time and when the audiences were falling off night after night you couldn't take any chances. He decided to cut out all of the spectacles and put Dorothy back into the line. He wasn't afraid of her. He knew that there wasn't anything in her contract. He knew that she was young and that the only power she had was a forgotten attachment to Golden. One night after the show he called the whole company back and described the changes he was going to make. When he had finished Dorothy came up to him.

"Do you think you're going to take out all of my numbers," she said, "and put me back in the line?"

"That's it."

"But you can't do that. You know you can't do that."

"Why can't I?"

"Because Mr Golden didn't give you the authority."

"But we're in Illinois and Mr Golden's in New York."

"I signed up with this show as the Princess Nika and I'm not going to do or be anything else."

"Well, in that case I guess you better find yourself another job."

"That's exactly what I'll do. Good night."

He knew that she couldn't get another job around there and he expected her to come back to him and he would be glad to put her in the line. But she didn't come back. Three days went by and they didn't see anything of her. Bacon began to worry. He knew she was broke and in a strange city and he remembered the way she had asked him to call her Princess that night in Philadelphia and it reminded him of her character and that she might be willing to go through with anything in order to keep up her estimation of herself. Finally, the day before the show moved on, he asked a couple of the girls to go up to her rooming house and see if she wouldn't come back with them. The girls agreed and after the matinee they went up to the house. The landlady said that she was in. "She hasn't been out for two days," she said. "I'm glad someone's come to see her. I was getting worried."

The door to her room was open and they knocked and went in. She wasn't there. The room was so clean that it looked as if no one were living there. But her dressing things were on the bureau and her luggage was stacked by the door. They heard the sound of someone taking a bath in the adjoining bathroom and they went to the door and called her name.

"Dorothy. Is that you? Dorothy."

The splashing stopped.

"Listen, Dorothy, the show leaves town tonight and Bacon wants you to come back."

"My name isn't Dorothy," she said. "I'm the Princess Nika."

"Don't be a damned fool, Dorothy. You don't want to get yourself stranded out here in this place. You can starve to death. Honestly you can. Open the door."

"Tell Bacon I'll come back when he realizes who I am," she said.

"Don't be a damned fool. Anything's better than starving in this place. Open the door."

She didn't answer them. She went on taking her bath. One of them pounded on the door.

"Open the door, Dorothy. We can't talk to you with the door shut. Open it up."

She didn't answer. They tried the door but it was locked. They could hear her taking her bath. They tried to impress her, through the closed door, with the fact that the show was leaving town that night, and that the world was large, and that once she let go they might never see her again; but they couldn't impress her.

"Tell Bacon I'll come back when he realizes who I am," she said.

The New Republic
October 28, 1936

The Teaser

AFTER THAT LAST week in Boston, Harcourt decided to fire Beatrice. She was through. Even the gallery didn't clap for encores, whatever she gave them. Harcourt didn't want to do it, but she was fifty-two years old and she would have to realize sometime that younger women were going to take her place. He didn't want to do it because he knew it would nearly kill her. No one else would give her a job; at least not on the stage doing teasers and that was the only thing she could do. On the night he put the notice in her pay envelope, he watched her from the back of the house. It confirmed his decision. Her face and figure were still good, but she had lost the trick. In growing older she had grown more confident and proud until she didn't make any effort to put it over. She made the house feel like dirt. After the intermission he went downtown. He wasn't going to be around when she got the news. She was a strong woman, still handsome, and she'd put up a fight. So he went downtown to a movie.

That was on Saturday night. After the show there was a rehearsal. The two leading comedians knew that Beatrice was through and somehow the girls had found out about it. After they were paid they stood around the stage waiting for Cohen to call the rehearsal and waiting for Beatrice to climb the iron stairs that wound up from the dressing-rooms and make the noise everyone expected her to make. For once there was no jealousy. They were not only sorry; they were frightened. None of the girls liked Beatrice. She never got along with the other women and never called the girls by their names. They stood around waiting, with their coats over their costumes, their tarnished dancing shoes showing. They felt as if they were responsible for her middle age. As if they ought to apologize.

They heard her running up the iron treads as she always came up those stairs. She was dressed in street clothes and she looked nice. She was carrying a big leather purse under one arm.

Instead of saying anything she walked right through the wings, right by the mail rack and out the door. From the window someone saw her hailing a cab. She looked as if she meant business. She might have something on Harcourt that would make him keep her. Cohen called the rehearsal and the girls lined up. A little after midnight, Harcourt came back and went up to Cohen, who was standing by the piano.

"What did Beatrice do?" he asked.

"She didn't do anything. She just got into her street clothes and went out."

"Oh, God. That's worse," Harcourt said. "She probably thinks she can sue me. She probably thinks she has something on me. But she hasn't. She hasn't anything on me."

ON SUNDAY THE whole show moved up to Portland by bus and they opened with a matinee on Monday. All the time Harcourt kept expecting to hear from Beatrice, but nothing happened. He didn't believe she would take it quietly. Her place was being taken by a younger girl named Marie Badu. She was a dark French-Canadian with a long build and swarthy skin. The orchestra played muted, rapid music and after the first encore she raced around the stage giving them all of it before they knew what they were seeing.

It was in January and there was a heavy snow on the ground. The girls were complaining about the snow and the cold all the time. They couldn't seem to heat the theatre and the air in the dressing-rooms and on the stage was stale and cold. It was an old house that was only opened two or three times a season and it smelt of camphor and disinfectant. After the first two nights the audience fell off. The gallery was always full but across the footlights and through the smoke you could see blocks of empty seats on the floor and no one ever sat in the boxes.

Marie Badu was leaving the theatre after the last show on Wednesday. She was quiet and she took her work seriously and she didn't talk with the line girls. She was walking up the alley that led from the stage door to the street. The eaves of the theatre overhung the sidewalk and the melting snow from the roof had frozen again on the paving. She stepped carefully in her high-heeled shoes, but halfway down the walk she slipped. Her left foot went forward and she fell, bending her right leg backwards from the knee. Some of the girls, coming out a few minutes later, found her there by the wall.

"Oh, for God's sake," she said softly, when they stopped. "Oh, for God's sake, don't stand around like a lotta saps, do something. I'm sorry," she added quickly, "but it hurts, it hurts. It hurts." One of the girls called a cab and they took her to a hospital. Her right leg was broken.

Harcourt didn't know what to do. They only had one other teaser in the show and one wasn't enough. It would take a girl a day and a night to come on from New York. There was no one in Boston but Beatrice. He didn't want to see her again. He was afraid to see her. He decided to try out one of the line girls. He took the prettiest one, a plump, fresh-looking blonde and rehearsed her all morning. She was anxious to get ahead and she was willing to do anything. But she couldn't seem to fall into it. She was slow and even shy. Harcourt stood in the back of the dark, dead theatre and shouted at her until he was hoarse.

"Give it to 'em. Shake it up. You're not here

to embarrass them."

"Yes, Mr Harcourt."

He put her on for the matinee, but when he went back to the office he wired Beatrice's hotel and called her to Portland.

They were buying tickets for the last show when she came into the office. She was wearing her black street clothes and she looked smart. Her face was pale and just enough bleached hair showed under her hat.

"What do you want?" she said.

"Now listen, Beatrice. I'm in a bad way. Sit down, sit down. Marie broke her leg on the ice in the alley and I'm short a girl. I want you to go on for me."

"You mean you want me to go on for the rest of the week?"

"That's it."

"Well, I'm not going to," she said quietly.

"Now listen, Beatrice. I'm in a bad way. With only one other girl we'll go so much in the red that it'll take us a month to pull out. I've done some bad things to you. I've done some good things. If you'll just do this for me."

"I'm not signing up for any three-day appearances. I'm not a substitute yet. The round trip up here cost six dollars. That's on you. Give me the money and I'll take the train back tonight."

"Now listen, Beatrice."

"If you want me to sign up for the rest of the season it's all right. But not for any three days. I know you think I'm through. You think I'm an old woman, don't you? Don't you? But I'm not. I can give it to them as well as any other girl on this circuit."

"How about a hundred dollars for the three days?"

"I tell you I'm not signing up for any three-day appearances whatever you pay me. Give me the six dollars. If you keep me here arguing I'll miss the train and it'll cost you a hotel bill."

Although Harcourt had pushed a chair toward her she was still standing.

"Well, suppose we call the three days a trial, then. You go on for three days and if they like you I'll keep you on for the rest of the season."

"If I make good I'll be on for the rest of the season?"

"Yes, you'll be on for the rest of the season."

She looked straight at him. Her eyes were

clear and her features were firm and pleasant. She looked fifty-two, but she was still attractive. Her figure was mature and athletic. The black dress gave her dignity. She looked like a widow.

"I won't make you sign any papers," she said. "I'll take your word for it. If you'll show me where the dressing-rooms are I'll go on before the intermission."

When she went on Harcourt was standing in the wings watching her and so were all the girls. They knew that something like a trial was up. She came in from the right on slow music. She was wearing a white evening dress that trailed on the floor. Her bleached hair shone in the light. She came up to the footlights and sang her song and then, to slower music, began to walk idly, proudly, around the stage, loosening the dress at her breasts. She had a quiet, wise smile on her face as if she knew everything in the world.

When she came off the indifferent applause sounded from backstage like someone spilling a pail of water. She went on again, under a pink light, her head lifted, the quiet, wise smile on her face. She knew her stuff and each exit was timed perfectly. On the third encore she had taken off everything but her skirt and she had this draped tightly around her body like a shawl. She came up to the footlights and dropped this onto the floor. The house was dead silent. A couple of men lighted cigarettes. Then she walked to the back of the stage and turned around. Harcourt was watching her all the time. The orchestra leader knew what she wanted and the drum began a brutal, monotonous beat. She lifted her arms, locked her hands at the back of her neck and began to buck.

It brought the house down. Harcourt had never heard a noise like that. From the wings it sounded like a heavy rain and thunder and above it you could hear them whistling from the gallery. He didn't know what she was doing until Cohen, who had been standing in the back of the house, came running up to him.

"God, she's wonderful," he said. He was laughing and breathing so heavily that he could hardly speak. "She's had someone paint a coupla red hands on her fanny. She's wonderful."

Instead of laughing with Cohen, Harcourt acted as if he hadn't heard, and walked away. He walked through the flats, out by the mail-rack, away from the clapping and the stamping. He walked out into the cold alley and stood there feeling as if he had sat beside her on all those desperate days and nights when she had sat in her hotel room, thinking it up, watching the traffic below her window.

The New Republic
September 8, 1937

His Young Wife

WHEN JOHN HOLLIS married a young girl he was probably the only one who was conscious of the difference in their ages. Sue was too young and impulsive to be conscious of anything like that and, anyway, in the beginning they were very happy together. There had been times, later on, when John had wondered if Sue would ever notice his age. Simple and meaningless things like the people they knew, the music they had danced to and the football games they remembered would remind him of their differences. "You dance like a cattle rancher, darling," she used to tell him and then she would go off and dance with younger men. But when the music had ended she would leave her partner and walk through the tables looking for him as if he were the only man in the smoky room. It had been like that, at least until she met Rickey. And then what had been an idle speculation and an apprehension for John became a literal and shaking fear. Skiing, he thought, had never given him a more headlong sense of terror and descent than he found in watching the happiness of Rickey and his young wife talking and smoking at the table in front of him.

The three were sitting at a table of the café in Belmont Park. Neither John nor Sue had ever seen a race until Rickey, through a casual business acquaintance, entered their lives. But after that you might have seen them at Belmont on any weekend during the meet, and on weekdays, when John was working, Rickey drove Sue out there himself. Her absorption in horse racing and Rickey, John thought, seemed inseparable. Once, in the beginning, John had spoken to her about going to the races so often with Rickey. "But I'm young, darling," she had said. There was a trace of petulance in her voice. "And I've never had a good time. Mother never let me out of her sight until I married you and I want to do something exciting before I grow too old."

From where they sat they had a good view of

the track. Rickey and Sue were at the front of the table with their backs turned to John and with an absorption in each other, he thought; with a happiness and a resentment of his presence that were as palpable as the smoke from their cigarettes. "Which is our horse?" Sue was asking. She was a young girl with white skin and yellow hair that seemed nearly brassy when the sun touched it.

"Top horse," Rickey said. "Bold Ransome. Isn't she a beauty?" He leaned across the table to point out his choice on her program. Their shoulders touched and John felt that anger and jealousy come up into his throat again. He watched them stand and adjust their glasses and follow their choice with a tenderness, he thought, that was like the tenderness of young parents. He was distracted a little from his anger by the marshal's bugle and he rose to watch the field walk down toward the barrier. The spring sun was strong and hot and the horses cast a long, running shadow on the turf as they passed.

THERE WAS NO disturbance and a moment later

there was that confused roar from the stands
and they could see the field streaking down
the backstretch and the dust coming up off
the track like smoke. Rickey's horse was third
and at the far turn she moved up to second.
"Comeon, Bold Ransome," he was yelling.
"Comeon, comeon, comeon, win for the hell of
it . . . ." But at the second turn she went wild,
running across the track to the outside rail and
by the time they came down the home stretch
she had lost her speed and her position. Rickey
sank tiredly into his chair and passed his hand
over his forehead as if he had a headache. "It's
crazy," he said. "The whole thing's crazy." There
was sincere worry and confusion in his voice.
"I've never lost as much on a meet before," he
said. "If I don't win pretty soon I won't be able
to get to Saratoga. I won't have the gasoline."
But his sadness was only momentary and before
they had posted the winners he rammed his program into his pocket and stood. He was a young
man but the intensity and anticipation of an incorrigible gambler had already begun to line his
face. "I guess I'll go down and shop around," he
said to Sue. "Want to come?" He still asked for

her company in a casual way as if he were conscious of John's proprietary rights.

"Sure," she said. "Love to." She couldn't conceal the happiness in her voice. "Want to come, John?" she asked dutifully, turning to her husband. "Want to come and put some money on a horse?"

"No, darling," John said; "you know I never bet."

"I know," she said a little tiredly. Then she picked up her purse and her gloves and took Rickey's arm and they worked their way through the tables toward the betting ring. He might be tied to her by string, John thought, for the singular sense of loss, even of pain, that he felt when she walked away from him.

After they had gone he called a waiter and ordered a sandwich and some coffee. He was acutely conscious of the happiness his wife was enjoying without him and it was easy for him to imagine them going around the paddock like a couple of young kids, which was, after all, what they were. Stirring and sweetening his coffee, he thought about the growth and the nature of their love for each other that was gradually imperiling his world. He had first become conscious of it that night, he remembered, when he had come home from work and found them sitting together in the dark garden, singing the dance music they remembered, tunes like "Star Dust" and "Limehouse Blues" and "After You've Gone." He had stood there at the door, listening to their thin voices and for an instant he had felt like an intruder. It wasn't the music he remembered. All he could remember was "Dardanella," and they would have laughed at him if he had tried to sing that. And then there had been that other evening when they had given a party and Rickey had been there. After all the guests had left, he and Sue didn't dance around the living room as they used to and sing: "They've gone, they've gone, they've gone." Instead of that she had sat quietly in a chair, talking about Rickey, about the things he had said and done as if she missed him more than she enjoyed the presence of her husband, as if he had taken some part of her with him, as if that life when they had danced around and laughed and sung after their guests had gone was coming to a close.

After that she had begun to talk about Rickey all the time. She talked about his unhappy marriage and his divorce. She talked about his extravagant mother, who was spending all of his money so that his allowance was cut down to nearly nothing, and about how lonely his life must be going from hotel to hotel or staying in other people's houses. "Sympathy," John thought, "seems to be the nature of her affection, but it's as strong as any other attachment. If the worst comes to the worst, I wonder how they'll break the news to me." If it would be Rickey he could imagine him coming into the room and bracing his shoulders as he often did. "I'm through with the horses," he would have said. "I'm tired of all that and I want to settle down and Sue's the only person I want to settle down with. We're happy together. We love each other terribly. I know it isn't kind or considerate or honorable but I haven't seen enough of kindness or consideration or honor in my world to have taught me to sacrifice my only happiness for those principles." But if it were Sue, he knew, it would be something different. He might come into the bedroom some night and find her packing. "I'm sorry, darling," she would have said, "but I'm crazy about him." It would have been something as simple as that and then he would have let her go. And realizing how true and imminent his fears were, he struck the table and swore under his breath and felt his eyes smarting.

WHEN THEY CAME back he might not have been sitting at the table for the attention they paid him.

"That's our horse," Rickey said, turning his shoulder a little and pointing out a horse. "That's our horse, Number Eight. The bay mare. Green silks." Our horse, John thought, our house, our car, our wife.

There was a big field that time and a long wait at the barrier and the crowd grew nervous. Then there was that confused roar and a woman near them began screaming: "Comeon, you Barfly! Comeon, you Barfly! Comeon, you Barfly! Comeon, you Barfly! . . ." But the crowd was generally still, still enough for them to hear the sweet drumming of hoofs on the backstretch. Then more people began to call out like the noise of a crowd coming nearer and nearer, street by street, and Rickey was shouting: "Tarvola, Tarvola, Tarvola," and bringing his fist down through the air again and again as if it held a crop. But his horse came in outside the money and before the roar in the stands had quieted he sat down and called a waiter and ordered a drink. "Look on a broken man, children," he said, lifting his drink. John noticed how his hand trembled. "Look on a man without a cent in the world. A man whose debts if they were placed from end to end would even surprise his father. I'm broke," he said seriously, "stone-broke, done up. It's never been like this before. I've lost money but I've never lost all of it."

"I'm sorry," Sue said, "terribly sorry." She spoke to him with the tenderness and understanding that John had thought of as the most beautiful thing in his experience until he saw it directed toward another.

"If I only had something to put on the next race . . ."

"Can I lend you something?" John asked.

"Would you mind?"

"Not at all. Would fifty be enough?"

"Wonderful. Would you put it on a horse for me? You might bring luck. On War-Bridge. At the best price."

"Sure," John said a little resentfully. He pushed

his chair back and started toward the betting ring.

For a moment after he had gone, there was that sweetness they always felt when they were left alone.

"I'm low," Rickey said.

"It's rotten luck." Her voice was soft.

"If it weren't for you," he said, "I don't know where I'd be. Honestly, darling, if it weren't for you I don't know where I'd be tomorrow morning. I've lost money before but I've never lost it like this and if I didn't have you to think about I guess I'd go crazy. I guess I'm through with the horses. I guess it's no good. I guess I want to live like other people. I want to live like you. I'm crazy about you. I think about you all the time; when I'm reading, when I'm walking, when I'm riding. . . ."

Then he began to talk about his marriage and the divorce. The experience had left him so embittered, he said, that he hadn't thought he could fall in love again until he met Sue. Then he talked about how tired he was of living in hotels and other people's houses and following the horses up and down the country. He was so absorbed in his talk that he hardly rose to watch the race, as if he already knew it were lost, and when his horse came in third he laughed and went on talking sadly about himself.

John was gone a long time. She was facing the track so she couldn't see him when he returned but she knew he was coming because Rickey took his hand off hers.

"Did you put it on the nose?" Rickey asked.

"I didn't put it on War-Bridge at all. I had a hunch and put it on Jamboree. And you won." Taking some bills out of his pocket, he counted them onto the table. "One hundred, two hundred, three hundred. . . ."

"But it's not my money," Rickey said.

"Sure it's your money," John said quietly. "I never bet."

"You mean it's mine?"

"It's yours."

"Oh, let me at 'em," Rickey said, pushing his chair back; "let me at 'em."

He doubled his money on the next race and he cleared a little more on the next. It was the first time he had won in several weeks and the change in his nature was complete. His absorption in his good luck was so great that he seemed to notice neither John nor Sue and he even seemed to show some contempt for their qualities of respectability that he had been coveting an hour earlier. He refused their invitation to dinner and he kept waving to people whose acquaintance he seemed to have rediscovered with his winnings. After the races were over and while they were walking across the lawns to the parking space, all he could talk about was Saratoga. Then he saw some more people he knew and he left John and Sue to talk with them. He kept them waiting a long time before he turned and called: "Don't bother to wait for me. I'll go back with someone else. And, oh," he said, as if he had just remembered something, "in case I don't see you again, thanks a thousand times for everything. You've been awfully kind. I'm going up to Saratoga on Thursday. I'll see you in the fall. I'll be back here in the fall." Then he went back to talking with the people he knew.

DRIVING BACK INTO the city the traffic was heavy and John and Sue said very little. John left Sue at the door and put the car away and when he came into their apartment he found her in the kitchen, mixing herself a drink. "Got a terrible chill at the races," she was telling the cook. "Got a terrible chill." When she saw John she looked up to him with something that seemed like fear. "Kick me," she said, when they were alone in the living room. "It's your prerogative, darling, to kick me."

"I don't want to kick you," he said.

She sat down and sighed and tasted her drink.

"It's lucky Rickey won that money," she said. "Do you know how lucky it is Rickey won that money?"

"Sure," he said. "I know how lucky it is Rickey won that money. Because he didn't win it. I gave it to him. Out of my own pocket. And I would have let him think he'd won a lot more if he needed any more to make him forget you. I figured I'd rather have you than any amount of money."

She put down her drink and walked over to where he was standing and when he took her in his arms she began to cry. Her sobbing was hard and quick like the breathing of a person who is tired. But it didn't hurt him because he knew she wasn't crying out of longing or fear or regret or pain or any of those things that would have hurt him if they had been the cause of her tears. She stayed in his arms for a long time, crying like a young kid over the rediscovery of her own immense happiness.

Collier's
January 1, 1938

Saratoga

WHEN ROGER GAIGE came down to the track that morning and told everyone, the trainers, the stableboys and railbirds, that he was going to change his way of living, a lot of them laughed openly and MaGrath, his best friend, couldn't conceal a smile. For fifteen years then they had been seeing his pleasant and unusually credulous face in every race-track paddock in the country and their inability to separate Roger from the paddocks was only a natural weakness of the human imagination. And when Roger made the change for what it was worth and did those things he had been threatening to do for fifteen years the story became as common around the Saratoga bars and bonfires as Man O'War's twenty-one-foot stride or the night Sam Shestov put thirty thousand dollars down on the craps table at Interlaken.

Walking out Union Avenue on a hot night that August, you could hear some stableboy building up to the climax of the story in phrases and details that were already familiar to everyone who listened. It wasn't their story, of course. They played no part in it. But nearly every minute of Roger's acquaintance with Judith Bereston had been seen by at least one pair of eyes, and the taxi drivers, the touts, the bookies and barmen easily pieced it together. They even changed Roger's name from "Twenty-to-one" to "New-way-of-life" and, hard as it was to remember and awkward to shout, that was the way they hailed him for a good many months afterward.

One thing no one could figure out was why Roger and Judith hadn't met before. Roger's father was one of the best-known plungers of the nineteenth century. Since he never played a horse with odds at less than eight-to-one and since he often played shots as long as twenty-to-one, that had been his nickname and Roger had inherited the name and the trait. Judith's father had been a plunger too. The fact that he owned a couple of platers made him seem a little more respectable, but it hadn't kept him from dying in debt. Both Roger and Judith had lost their mothers: one by divorce and the other by death. Both of them had been brought up in racetracks and both had touched the fringes of a wealthy society.

Once, when Judith's father was flush, she had been sent to an expensive school; but that lasted only a couple of months and the next thing she knew she was being farmed out in a convent on Staten Island. It had been the same with Roger, and as far back as he could remember his life had been alternately rich and poor, sustained by the indestructible anticipation and faith of a gambler.

Judith had made a few changes in the way of living she inherited. Roger had made none. He had a small income and he lived exactly as his father had expected him to, following the horses up and down the country, moving, at times, among people of wealth, and convincing himself by one deceit or another that he was lucky, rich and contented. Sometimes he came to the Saratoga meet by air. Sometimes he came by train or boat or bus. Sometimes he hitchhiked, and once he had covered the distance between Ballston and Saratoga on foot.

Everything he did he did in the several ways of

the very rich and the very poor. Sometimes he slept in the big hotels and sometimes he slept on the strip of lawn that divides Union Avenue, wrapped up in copies of the *Morning Telegraph*.

They might have met when they were children. Their backgrounds were identical. They moved in an unusually small world. But something kept them apart and Roger was twenty-seven and she was twenty-five by the time they met. That was the night after Montola won the Clonmell, paying twenty-to-one. It was Roger's first profitable bet in nine days of racing.

THAT NIGHT ROGER went up to the casino. He felt fine. His pockets were full of money and he felt that one long shot meant a streak of luck. The craps tables he passed in the outer room were crowded. The shaded, overhead lights doubled the avidity of the players' faces and the air seemed literally to smell of money. He passed through that room into a farther one where roulette was being played. Here the crowd was quieter and better dressed. But there were the same avid faces, the same reek of tobacco smoke, and that same quick smell that might have been the smell of money. He took a vacant place at one of the tables. Those around him had expressionless faces, and they were shrewd enough to distinguish, in his face, his yellow hair and the deep lines in his forehead, the features of an incorrigible plunger. He played fifty dollars' worth of chips, and quietly, mercilessly, the croupier raked them off.

He had been playing for about twenty minutes when he felt someone's eyes on him. Turning, he noticed the girl beside him. She glanced away quickly and put some chips on a number. She was young, he thought. She was blond with nice eyes and striking white shoulders and clothing that might have meant money. A few minutes later he heard her voice. She hadn't turned her head; her voice was low and, although she spoke to him as if she were trying to conceal the fact from someone, he knew she was speaking to him.

"Do me a favor?" she asked.

"Yes."

"Take me home?"

"Sure."

Before he had time to pass any more money on to the banker she had taken his arm and they were walking through the tables toward the door. They looked well together. They looked as if they might have known each other for years. A collection of taxis and carriages stood out in front and they climbed into a carriage.

"Where do you live?" he asked her.

"The United States Hotel."

"Want to go around the park first?"

"All right."

"Around the park," he told the driver. With a lurch and a creak of wheels the carriage started off. It moved slowly through the heavy traffic of Saratoga's main street.

"Cigarette?"

"Thanks," she said.

In the matchlight he saw her pleasant and young face again.

"What's your name?" he asked.

"Judith. Judith Bereston. What's yours?"

"Roger Gaige."

"Oh," she said. "I think my father knew your father."

"Really?"

For some time neither of them spoke. The clop-clop of the horses' hoofs filled the silence. Roger put his arm around her. Even the driver started when he heard the crack of her hand across Roger's face.

"All right," Roger said, "all right."

"Did I hurt you?"

"I don't think so." He wiped his face with a handkerchief. A ring she was wearing had torn the skin and there was a little blood.

"Why did you ask me to take you home?"

"Because you were losing money," she said quietly. "If you hadn't come out of there with me you would have lost every cent you have."

"Girl Scout?" he asked.

"No," she said. "Campfire Girl."

"Don't you know," he asked angrily, "that when a man's over twenty-one years old he can do what he wants with his money? Who's going to get out of this carriage first—you or I?"

"I am," she said. "Driver," she called, "will you stop?"

The carriage creaked to a stop. She climbed out and began walking across the park.

"Hey, wait a minute, wait a minute," Roger

shouted. "Judith, Miss Bereston, wait a minute, wait. . . ." But it was dark and she had gone out of sight and after having missed each other for fifteen years that was the way they met.

WHEN ROGER WOKE up the next morning in the rooming house across from the track where he lived, he felt awful. His mouth was furred; his head was throbbing. Hangovers and their remorse were nothing new for Roger. Next to a gambler's faith in ultimate success, remorse was one of the things he knew best. And although he had never made any effort to change his way of living he thought continually of the better worlds in which other men lived, of country houses and steady jobs, of wives and children. He could see the house he wanted then. White. It was always white. It was not far from a trout stream and yet not too far from the ocean. And he was walking up from the stream with a creel full of trout and his wife was standing on the porch, waving to him, and the smell of coffee was drifting out of the open windows. Roger had been married once.

His wife had left him after six months, amiably enough, but fed up with horses.

He was miserable. When he went out to watch the trial runs he still felt miserable. It was something stronger than the pleasant and resigned melancholy he felt when he thought of the house, the wife and the trout stream. It was something that might, if he persisted, force him to act.

He watched the races from the clubhouse that afternoon, making his bets between the clubhouse and the grandstand. Between the third and the fourth races he went into the bar. When he came out he saw her standing there on the stretch of grass between the terrace and the track. She was standing there, just standing there looking at a horse at the barrier. She had on something white, a plain dress that any other woman at the track might have been wearing. There was a man beside her, short and swarthy and old enough to be her father. Without thinking Roger went over to speak to her.

"Good afternoon."

She put down her glasses and turned. She colored. "Hello," she said.

"I'm sorry about last night," he said.

"That's all right," she said.

"Can I see you again?"

That was the crisis, he knew. And he saw some indecision in her face. Then she answered him as directly, as simply as he had made the question. "You can see me tonight," she said, lowering her voice. "You can pick me up at the casino at ten."

Then she turned back to watching the barrier as if a stranger had asked her for a match or the time of day. And Roger, knowing what was good and what was enough and that there was a time for everything, walked away.

He went up to the casino that night at ten. He found her playing at the same table. When she saw him she cashed in her chips and put on her wrap and they went out. "Want to go to Riley's?" he asked her. "Want to go out to Arrowhead?"

"No," she said. They were on the street in front of the casino then. "I'm tired," she said. "I want you to walk me back to the hotel."

"You mean I'm going to walk you back to the hotel and say good night?"

"If you don't want to," she said, "I can take a cab."

That humbled him. "All right," he said, "but I don't see why."

She took his arm warmly. They walked down through the crowd.

"I was awfully glad to see you this afternoon," he said. "I felt low all morning; I felt awfully low. I didn't know what it was. I didn't . . ."

"I was glad to see you," she said.

Ahead of him then he could see the bulk of the United States Hotel, as homely and lonely and large in that small town as the abandoned cotton mills you see in Maine.

"You won't change your mind?" he said. "You won't have a drink with me?"

"No," she said, "I'm tired. Perhaps tomorrow night."

He could have kicked himself for the pleasure he showed. They were standing then by the entrance of the hotel.

"The same place, the same time?"

"Yes," she said, "and thanks." She gave him her hand. "Good night."

She turned and went up the stairs and he saw her disappear in the crowded lobby.

HE CALLED FOR her the next night. She said she
was still tired and all he could do was walk her
back to the hotel. He had promised himself that
if she tried this again he would let her walk
home alone. But in her presence he forgot his
resolution and he was up at the casino the next
night and the night after that. On the fourth night
he kept his promise to himself and lost his temper. "I'm dammed if I'm going to be used for an
escort," he said. "Why don't you hire a detective?
Why don't you take a taxi? Why don't you . . .?"
Then the tone of his voice changed. "Won't you
at least go for a ride?" he asked.

"Of course," she said simply.

They were in front of the casino. The carriage
that had taken them home the first night was
there. They climbed in and she was the one who
told the driver to go out Union Avenue. When
they turned off the brightly lighted main street
he put his arm around her. She leaned back in
his arms like a person who is tired. "I'm crazy
about you," he said. She didn't slap him. She
didn't wisecrack. She answered in the voice of a
person who is tired. "I'm crazy about you," she
said.

Their carriage passed a lighted hotel, some empty school buildings. A party was in full swing in a house on Union Avenue they passed. They could hear people talking and laughing and the mechanical thumping of a piano. The driver listened carefully to the conversation of his fares.

"There are some things I ought to tell you," she was saying. "My father was a gambler. Like yours. Mother died and he started taking me around to the tracks when I was young. I got used to it. That was about the only thing I ever did get used to. And then when he died I just went on going around to the tracks because it was the only thing I knew. I'm a fool. You may as well know that in the beginning. Once, when I had some money, I owned a couple of horses. I can't seem to keep away from them. Sometimes I make money. Mostly I don't. But I know so many people now that when I'm in the red I can usually pick up a job.

"I model clothes at the track every afternoon for the man you saw me with. And then at night I work up at the casino. I go there at six and play until ten. I'm a shill. There isn't much doing between six and ten and they figure a woman at the tables will lead the suckers on. That's what I am. That's what I do. Are you disappointed? Did you think I was Mrs Astor?"

"Why should I be disappointed?" he asked. "I don't even work as a shill. My father left me a little money and I play it. Sometimes I win and I live in style and sometimes I lose and I live like any bum. But I don't mind being poor because I'm always sure it won't last. It's a lie. I know it's a lie. It's crazy."

Up until then both of them had thought of their experiences as singular. But, talking together that evening, they found they had been identical. They knew the same hotels and people and places. They knew the same sensations, the excitement of winning and the remorse of loss and debt. They had both dodged landladies and hocked jewelry and borrowed. Their confidence, their familiarity with each other was something neither of them had experienced before.

Their carriage passed the racetrack. The driver noticed that his fares had stopped talking. It was not until they had come back onto Union Avenue that he heard their voices again.

"We ought to get married," Roger was saying.

His voice was husky and low like the voice of a man who has just been awakened. "Neither of us likes the way we live. If we don't do something about it, we'll die like this. I'll be an old man hobbling around the paddock. You'll be old too. You'll be one of those old women with a purse full of dope sheets." He laughed. "If we get together maybe we could reform. We could buy a house and live in it. For years and years.

"It's a lie," he said, "the way we live. We spend ninety percent of our energies planning to spend money we'll never have. We could help each other. We could change. We could spend our money for something besides whiskey and flowers. We could buy a house."

"What would we buy it with?" she asked.

"I've got a little money," he said. "I'll play it tomorrow. On Espion. I'm sure of her and the price ought to be good. If she wins we'll get married. We'll leave the track for good. We'll buy a house. Is it a go?"

The driver didn't know if she was laughing or crying.

"It's a go," she said.

The old horse, anxious to return to the stables,

broke into a trot as they approached the village.

IT WAS ON the next morning that Roger went around the track, saying goodbye. "If Espion wins," he told MaGrath, "I'm going to quit the horses and get married and settle down. I'm going to change my way of life." Those were the words he used and they sounded awkward and mealy to his friends. The stableboys laughed and chuckled and instead of hailing him as "Twenty-to-one" they began that morning to call him "New-way-of-life."

There was nothing funny about that afternoon for either of them. It was a sober and important occasion in which there was hardly room for talk. They took a table and sat down. She ordered a vermouth. They said the things people say under stress. He asked her if she had eaten lunch, if she had read the paper, if she wanted a cigarette. "I told my boss I might be getting through tomorrow," she said. She rapped on the table. "He laughed. He thought it was funny."

"I told MaGrath," Roger said. "I told MaGrath I was getting through. He thought it was funny, too."

When the winners were posted at the end of the third he got up without saying anything. She followed. He went down to the betting ring under the grandstand where he thought he might get a better price and she waited for him by the gates that lead to the paddock. He found the price, when he entered the crowd, up to twelve and fifteen. He waited five minutes, eight minutes, keeping his eyes on as many slates as possible. Then at the end of the long corridor formed by the bookie's desks he saw the price go up to twenty. He pushed his way through the crowd and put down his money. Walking away, he saw the price go back to fifteen, then twelve. He returned to where she was waiting and they went down to the paddock.

ESPION WAS A horse whose sire and grandsire had brought Roger money. Haughty and a little fractious, she was being saddled in the shadow of an elm. They stood together, feeling a warmth for that animal that approached love. They watched her being saddled. They watched the nervous jockey mount. They saw his frightened smile. "She'll win for us, she'll win for us, she'll win for us," ran through Roger's mind like a refrain. They felt their relation to that horse was something the chattering crowd around them would never be able to understand. Then they joined the crowd that was rushing back to the stands. They walked slower than the others. They didn't talk.

Espion was top horse. Number two was Moll Flanders. Lead Pencil, Count Astrov and Jolly Iris followed in order. There were twelve entries altogether. But when the field paraded past them a few minutes later Espion was the only horse they saw. "She's a beauty," Judith said. Roger rapped on wood. The wait seemed endless. Then the field wheeled about and galloped up toward the barrier. "Want a drink, darling?" she asked. She could see how nervous he had grown. He didn't reply. He shook his head and handed her the glasses. The horses were at the barrier then and a quiet had come over the crowd. In the unnatural silence they could hear the splattering of the fountain in the field; the yelling of some kids in a distant parking lot.

Then that roar of thousands shouting and rising to their feet broke on the hot afternoon. A cloud of dust rose up from the backstretch and they could hear, faintly, just faintly, the swelling drum of the field. At first the numbers were posted three, four, seven, then three, four, five, then three, four, one and then, at the turn, three went way off and it was five, one, seven and then Roger stood and began to yell and everyone around him was yelling and he was beating on the table yelling: "Espion, Espion, Espion, Espion, Espion . . ." and then Espion and Iris broke from the back and came neck and neck down the stretch and when she turned to tell him Espion had won she found him sitting at the table with his head buried in his arms.

"We can get married," she was shouting above the noise of the crowd. "We're going to get, we can get . . ." Then she noticed something unnatural about his position. In putting his arms on the table he had spilled her vermouth, the contents of an ashtray and scuffed up the linen with his elbows. "Roger!" she called, "Roger! Roger! Espion won! Roger!" She shook his shoulders. They were lifeless under her hands. He had fainted. He was out cold.

"BELOVED, WE ARE gathered here together," the minister said that evening. MaGrath, the trainer, and Malloy, the bookie, whom they had asked as witnesses, cleared their throats. They took the vows, Roger slipped a ring on her finger and it was all over. They said goodbye to MaGrath and Malloy on the steps of the church. The minister watched them go down the street together.

She checked out of the United States, he left his boardinghouse and they spent what they sometimes called their honeymoon in a modest hotel in the north end of town. They were very happy together and they talked continually about the change they had made. But the money they had won on Espion, lying idle in the bank, worried them both, and on the third day Roger decided to borrow MaGrath's car and drive out to the country to see if there was a house around there they might buy. He taxied out to the track that morning, coming in through the gates for the first time since his marriage.

MaGrath was in good humor. Blue Bottle was

running in the seventh that afternoon and he was sure of her and he would have given Roger his shirt. Roger didn't look around the track. He didn't dare. He knew how strong the temptation would be. He took MaGrath's car keys, thanked him and drove away. She was waiting for him at the hotel with some sandwiches and wine. The desk clerk told them the best road into the country and they left Saratoga behind them.

It was in Washington County somewhere, down near the Hudson, that they found what they wanted. It was a small white house on the water side of the road. Four simple pillars supported the porch roof. A lawn reached down to the banks of the Hudson. The doors were locked and the windows were shuttered, but they, or at least she, knew what the interior would be like. They would be able to see the river, the valley and the mountains of Vermont from their tall windows. Standing there on the lawn, she planned the color of the carpets, the wallpaper and arranged the rooms.

They ate their lunch in the shadow of a locust grove. She fell asleep and he sat beside her, listening to what were for him the strange noises of the country. A bird sang. A tree creaked in the wind. He left her and walked down to the bank and stripped and dove into the cool water. They might even have a boat, he thought while he swam, they could fish and and swim and sail all summer.

When he returned she was awake.

"It's nice," she said. Her voice was sleepy.

"Yes."

"It's nice and quiet. Listen to that bird. I wonder what kind of bird it is."

"I don't know."

"I love it," she said. "I've always loved the country."

"So have I," he said.

"What time is it?"

"Three-thirty."

For some time neither of them spoke. "A penny for your thoughts," she said.

"I was thinking," he said slowly, "that there must be some streams leading into the river. And that there must be some trout in the streams. And that . . ." His voice trailed off.

"Really?" she asked.

"No," he said tiredly. "I wasn't thinking about that at all. I was thinking that Blue Bottle is running in the seventh. And that it's a sure thing and that I wish I had some money running on her. That's what I was thinking."

"I thought so," she said.

"How did you know?"

"Because that's what I was thinking."

"We've got to stop it," he said angrily. He thumped the grass with his fist. He took her in his arms. "We've decided to change. We can. We will."

"Sure we will," she said. "It's just a habit. That's all. When we get back into Saratoga we'll go to the real-estate agent and ask him about this place. And we'll buy it before we spend the money for anything else. And we'll live in it."

But for some reason her voice lacked conviction. He realized resentfully how much a product of cities and crowds they were. In the silence he heard a sound, obscure, plaintive, a sound like the ringing of zinc. "We'd better start back," he said, "the races will be over and MaGrath will be wanting his car."

"Promise you won't put any money on Blue Bottle?" she asked.

"I promise," he said. "Cross my heart."

BACK IN SARATOGA he let her off at the hotel. His intentions, until he drove out Union Avenue anyhow, had been sincere. But the closer he came to the track the greater the conflict in his mind became until his thinking lost all coherence and became a series of meaningless resolutions and profane oaths. When he drove into the track the horses were lined up at the six-furlong barrier. That meant it was the sixth and he gave a sigh of relief. As he climbed out of the car he heard the roar of "They're off!" from the grandstand; but he didn't look, he didn't watch that race. He was searching the small gathering at the rail and in the field for a bookie's runner.

When he saw one of Malloy's men he asked him the price on Blue Bottle. It was eight-to-one. He gave him a hundred dollars. Then, cracking his fingers and swearing under his breath, he walked back and forth in the road, scuffing up dust. If he lost, he thought, he wouldn't tell her. And if he won he wouldn't tell her either. The less she knew about that angle of his character the better. And this was the last time. And since it was going to be the last time there was no reason why he should tell her. They would buy that house, that white house on the Hudson with the pillars out in front.

In order to calm himself he went up onto MaGrath's porch. MaGrath was sitting there sucking at his pipe. Neither of them spoke. Across the field they could see the entries for the seventh being paraded. He couldn't distinguish Blue Bottle at that distance. Then the loose, lightly reined field rode up around the bend. They were fourteen and it took them ten minutes to make a start. When the bell rang, Roger started involuntarily. A noise like a roll of drums filled the air and the field rocketed down the backstretch, straining for the turn and then he could hear the screaming of thousands in the grandstand and then through the dust he lost the colors and the horses and miserably he covered his face with his hands. He heard the noise of the crowd abate, then swell again when the winner was posted. Opening his eyes, he saw the smile of contentment on MaGrath's face.

They had some drinks. It wouldn't have been right to go away. They drank to Blue Bottle, then to MaGrath, then to Blue Bottle again. It was eight o'clock and the sun was setting when he hailed a cab to take him back to the village. When he came into their room it was growing dark. There was a note on the bed. "Darling," it read, "I got tired of waiting. I've gone out to the yearling auctions. The Barstows are selling a filly and I like her and I want to see who she goes to and for how much. I'll see you out there. Love. Judith . . . ."

He washed, changed his shirt and hailed a cab on Broadway to take him out to the auction ring where the yearlings are sold.

THERE WAS A crowd there that night. Jockeys, touts and trainers were jammed outside the open pavilion. He pushed his way through the crowd looking for her. She was sitting in the reserved section flanked by a Philadelphia family and a half dozen movie stars. She can still get around, he thought. He climbed up the bleachers and sat down beside her.

"Hello."

"Hello there."

A filly was being led around in the ring below them. The glare of light was strong and the horse was nervous. "Ten hundred; who'll give me twelve?" the auctioneer was calling. "Ten hundred; who'll give me twelve? Ten hundred; who'll give me twelve?"

Collier's
August 13, 1938

The Man She Loved

MRS DEXTER OVERHEARD JOE ordering a pork chop. That was the way it began. The Dexters were late in going up to the diner and all of the tables were taken. The waiter gave them the three unoccupied chairs at Joe's table. They nodded to Joe in the way strangers nod to one another in a dining car and then everybody sat down and stared at the menu. The waiter returned a few minutes later and Joe ordered the pork chop. "But, young man, you shouldn't eat pork," Mrs Dexter told him, "you don't look at all well and you shouldn't eat pork — fried pork."

Lila broke the embarrassed silence that followed her mother's exclamation. "Tilly, darling," she said, "let the gentleman eat what he wants." She gave Joe an apologetic smile. "Yes, Tilly," Charles said, "it's really none of your business, you know." Then Joe changed his order from pork to calves' liver and that was how the Dexters met him. They spent the rest of the trip together in the club car. That was aboard the racetrack special pounding through the mill towns north of Albany on its way to Saratoga.

Joe Clancy was a good-looking Irishman with the apprehensive scowl of a man watching his horse falter on the stretch. Years of gambling had drawn four deep lines in his forehead that even sleep failed to erase. Mr and Mrs Dexter were a well-dressed middle-aged couple. Lila, their daughter, was not quite twenty. Her fine features, her long lashes and blue eyes were less noticeable than the impression of youth and spirit she gave. They were a confused and friendly family and when the train drew into Saratoga, Mrs Dexter told Joe: "It was very nice to have met you. We'll see you at the track tomorrow, and come up to the hotel for dinner on the first evening you're free." Then she turned and began to wave at a policeman and to call: "Redcap! Redcap! Redcap!" She was quite nearsighted.

Twenty years earlier the Dexters had made the trip from the Saratoga depot to the Grand

Hotel in an open carriage. It had been partly to commemorate this trip that they had returned. In the intervening years they had seen a great deal of change. On their first trip they had been people of wealth and position. Personal extravagance and reckless speculation had reduced them to living in a modest apartment off the income Charles made from selling cars.

Lila had finished secretarial school that spring and was going to work in the fall. Both her parents felt they owed her at least one glimpse of a world they had known rather well. They were giving it to her as a birthday present. It was largely for this reason that they were making a trip they could not afford into a world they had tried to forget.

"They haven't changed a thing," Mrs Dexter said that evening, gesturing around the dining room of the Grand Hotel. Lila noticed a dark-haired man approaching their table. "The same windows," Mrs Dexter rattled on, "the same decorations—"

She stopped speaking when she became conscious of someone standing at their table. It was the man Lila had noticed. Mrs Dexter gave him the rude stare of those who are very nearsighted. Then her face lighted. "Lord Devereaux! Lord Devereaux! How young you look! Why, how young you've grown! You've grown so much younger since I saw you last. You've—" She seemed confused. Then she began again with even more enthusiasm: "But you're not Percy Devereaux, are you? You're Napier Devereaux! Little Napier Devereaux! For a minute I thought you were your dear father. How you've grown! Napier, how you've grown! Charles! Charles, this is Napier Devereaux. My daughter, Lila."

The Englishman sat down at their table. He was a man in his thirties with a sharp, aristocratic face, a cleft chin and dark, wet hair. He waited for the Dexters to finish their coffee and he joined them after dinner on the veranda. "Isn't it extraordinary, meeting you up here?" Mrs Dexter was saying. "Of all the places in the world, of all the people! You're here for the races of course."

"No," Napier said quietly. "I abominate horse races. I'm up here to take the cure. To drink the waters. My physician recommends them. I've been to India y'know. Joined the Ragi cult. Done me worlds of good. Made a new man out of me."

"That sounds wonderful," Mrs Dexter said. "Doesn't that sound wonderful, Charles? Ragi. Mysterious."

"Mysterious in a way," Napier went on. "Based on a series of sound hygienic laws, though. Breathing exercises in the morning. Strict diet. No tobacco. Nothing worldly. Seat of the soul in the diaphragm and all that sort of thing."

"Lila, did you hear that?" Mrs Dexter asked. "Napier has joined the Ragi cult. I'm sure Lila would love to hear about the Ragi cult." She stood. There was something hurried about her departure that even she could not conceal. "Come along, Charles, come along. You know we have a lot to do. Let Napier tell Lila all about the Ragi cult. Good night, Napier. Good night, Lila." Then she disappeared into the lobby, followed by her confused husband.

Once upstairs Mrs Dexter spent a long time pacing the floor of her bedroom. She had begun to imagine a birthday present that was more spectacular and enduring than any month at Saratoga. Her days were numbered, she knew, and her funds were limited, but on her side was an old and distinguished family that would be as important to Napier as the color of Lila's eyes.

Fate was generous, she thought, and she felt her eyes smarting with tears. She had been dealt an unexpected hand and she knew exactly how to play it.

"THAT'S HIM, SIR," Joe whispered. "Look, Miss Dexter, look, that's Juan."

In Manhattan the milk wagons would still be making their rounds. It was very early. The wet grass spotted Lila's riding boots. The breath of the horses who were crossing the road and coming up toward the track smoked on the cool air. "Look, Miss Dexter, look," Joe whispered. "They sold him last year. For nine hundred dollars. I saw him in Havana. Look at his legs. Look at that chest. Did you ever see anything like it?"

They moved over to the rail. Juan, Joe's favorite, entered the track. He took two furlongs easily and then their hands tightened on the rail when they heard that faint, profound pounding rise up from the homestretch on the other side of the field. He was going then, rocketing down the track, pounding the loose dirt for everyone to hear. They eased him off again. "Nobody knows who he is," Joe said, "oh, glory be!"

"Where's Casanova?" Charles asked.

"Over there," Joe said, "the black one with the blinders."

"That's mine," Charles said, "that black one's mine."

"Aren't they beautiful, Miss Dexter?" Joe said. "Did you ever see anything as beautiful?"

The sun was higher. More and more horses, blanketed and bandaged like feudal mounts, were filing across the road. That was early in the second week of the Dexters' stay at Saratoga and Joe and Lila and Charles were already famil-iar figures at the morning workouts.

Mrs Dexter did not join them. She had her own work to do. She spent her morning walking up and down the drink hall of the spa with Napier, drinking a glass of saline water. She began with the long and distinguished history of her family. Then she turned her talk to more personal sub-jects. "Lila is such a lonely child, such a lonely and sensitive child," she said. "Of course you wouldn't think it to see her, but a great deal of her gaiety is bravado, sheer bravado. She feels that so few people understand her. She enjoys talking with you. She found you so different from the men, mere boys, that she knows."

"Really," Napier said.

"It's unkind of me," she said, "to burden you with my troubles. But I'm not a young woman any longer. And there are so few people I care to confide in. But I do worry about Lila. She needs someone to take care of her, someone understanding. Beneath all that gaiety is a great sadness and longing. She tries to conceal it from me. She's so considerate. But I know! I know!"

In the evenings Mrs Dexter saw that Napier and Lila were left together. She felt assured of the success of her work in Lila's frequent references to England and in the covetous and melancholy glances Napier gave her daughter.

Joe Clancy had rented a car for the month and he usually drove the Dexters out to the track. In those few weeks he had come to feel that he was a member of their family. It was a casual and unselfconscious relationship whose strength he would not know until it came time to say goodbye.

One day when Lila and Joe and Charles were in the paddock, Mrs Dexter accepted a dinner invitation for herself and her husband. She forgot it until the end of the seventh race. They were working their way out to the parking lot when she remembered the engagement. She and Charles were ahead. Lila and Joe were following. Tilly turned and called over the heads of the crowd: "You take Lila home, Joe. We're driving out with the Van Buskirks. For dinner. You eat dinner with Napier, darling. He'd like that. You take her home, Joe, take good care of her." Then her voice grew faint and she was carried off by the crowd.

The main road to town was choked with traffic and Joe took a back country road.

Do you want me to leave you at your hotel, Miss Dexter?" he asked.

"Don't call me Miss Dexter."

"All right," he said.

"My name is Lila," she said. "Call me Lila. And don't take me back to the hotel. Take me for a ride. A long ride." She slumped in the seat and crossed her legs and lit a cigarette.

Joe raced the car over the dirt roads of the Saratoga plain for some time before he spoke again. He finally mouthed a question: "What about Lord

Devereaux?"

"Oh, he'll be all right. He's not expecting me."
She moved closer in the seat to Joe. It was not a
flirtatious move. It was candid and friendly.
"Tell me about yourself," she said. "Tell me about
where you come from and what you want to do
and where you're going."

"I come from Chicago," he said abruptly. "I'm a
gambler. When I'm broke I wait on tables. I like
horses. I—" Then his voice lapsed into something that resembled static. "You don't want to
hear about me," he said.

They drove another five miles without speaking. They passed through a small village. When
they passed the saloon Lila made Joe stop.

"You don't want to go into a place like that,"
he said.

"Oh, yes I do," she said. He followed her and
she ordered drinks for both of them.

After a few beers Joe felt more at ease. He began to talk. He told her he was an orphan, that he
had worked as a stable boy, an exercise boy and
a bookie's runner and that he occasionally made
enough to live as a gambler. He had made a kill-
ing that spring in Belmont. He told her the story of

his life, that long history of rooming houses and misfortune, without an interruption. "I'm going to wait and see Juan run in the Holly stakes," he said, "and then, win or lose, I'm going to drop it all. It's a bad racket and I'm just beginning to see it. I'm fed up. I'm tired." His story ended as abruptly as it had begun.

They drove back in the dusk.

"What about Lord Devereaux?" Joe asked.

"Oh, I like him," Lila said. "He's very nice. Mother likes him too. As a matter of fact, I may marry him—if he asks me."

The sun had set. From the distance came the hooting of a train and the rumble of freight cars.

"Napier has a big house in England," Lila said. "Mother's been there. She liked it."

They crossed a bridge and at the next grade crossing they found the striped gates down, the lanterns still swinging. Then a locomotive rounded the bend. The freight cars passed slowly through the glare of Joe's headlights.

"Mother says his house has a moat around it," Lila was saying. "And it has two towers and—" She began to cry.

"What's the matter, kid?" Joe asked. "What's the

matter?" He put his arm around her shoulder. He was awkward.

"It's nothing. I was just thinking how lonely you must be. Never staying in one place. Traveling all the time. Oh, I'm stupid; I'm such a fool." She wiped her eyes with a handkerchief. The caboose rumbled past. The gates went up and they started back to town.

They finished the ride without speaking. She said good night to him in front of the hotel and there was something dry, something self-conscious in the way they spoke, the way they avoided facing each other.

"HOLD STILL," MRS DEXTER said, "hold still." She was tying her husband's black tie. "Stop sticking your neck out."

"I've got a hunch on that horse," Charles said, "the black one."

"Stop talking about horses," she said, "and tell me what Napier told you. You haven't told me a thing yet."

"Oh, he said the usual things. He said he thought he ought to tell me."

"Tell you what?"

"That he liked Lila. That he would consider it an honor to marry into your family. Does he know we're broke, by the way?"

"Of course he knows we're broke. Broke and well-connected. I've told him."

"Well, he said he would consider it an honor to marry into your family. He didn't say anything about my family. And he said he felt that he ought to tell me his intentions were serious. That's all."

She gave the tie a last touch and stepped away.

"That's fine," she said.

"I don't think it's so fine," he said. "I can't help it, darling, but I've never liked that sort of Englishman."

"I didn't mean that. I meant the tie. But I think it's fine about Napier too. It really is, Charles."

Mrs Dexter sat down at her dressing table and began to comb out her hair.

"That black devil," Charles said, "Casanova. I've got a hunch. I had a dream about him."

"Casanova who, dear?"

"The horse. The one that ran Tuesday. The big black one."

"Yes, it's fine," she said. "It will be such a nice change for Lila, living in England."

MRS DEXTER was patient. Morning after morning she discussed her distinguished antecedents. Napier told her he was tired of cattle millionaires and theatrical people and that her modest and well-born family was a relief. It was her best card with an English nobleman, she knew, and she played it shrewdly. In the third week her patience was rewarded. Napier told her the nature of his intentions and outlined his plans. He would cancel his passage to England and spend the fall and winter in New York. Their engagement could be announced after Christmas if Lila were willing, and they could be married in the summer. He asked Mrs Dexter to notify Lila and he arranged to meet them all at the hotel at four that afternoon for a discussion of the situation.

Returning to the hotel that morning, Mrs Dexter felt a happiness she had never known before. In the taxi she anticipated the scene over lunch when she would announce the good news. But when she hurried into their suite she found a note propped up on the parlor mantel. "Lunching with Joe," it read. "See you out at the track. Love. L." . . .

The usual things that delayed Mrs Dexter, the loss of her glasses and the fact that her watch had stopped, kept her from getting out to the track that afternoon in time for the first race. Charles had gone on ahead and when her taxi entered the grounds they were saddling the horses for the second. She gave the driver a large tip and hurried onto the terrace. Lila and Joe and Charles were sitting there quietly. "Hello, hello, hello," Mrs Dexter sang. Charles and Joe stood. "Hello, Charles. Hello, Joe. Hello, Lila. I expected to have lunch with you today, Lila. I have something very important to tell you. Vermouth, *un peu de* vermouth," she told the waiter. "What are you looking so glum about, Charles? And you, Joe. You look ill, both of you."

"Shall we go?" Charles asked Joe.

"All right."

"Wait a minute, wait a minute. Where are you going?"

"To bet."

"Well, wait a minute. I want to pick a horse. It's

no fun watching a race unless you have some money on it. Or is it?" She rapped the program with her glasses and scanned the entries. "Crepe," she said. "That's a pretty name. Don't you think that's a pretty name, Lila? Put two dollars on Crepe for me."

The two men walked off.

"WELL, WHAT ARE they looking so glum about?" Mrs Dexter asked.

"Oh, Dad has a hunch," Lila said. "A horse named Casanova. He's putting his bank book on the nose."

"But why should that make him glum?"

"I don't know. He's not sure. The price is too good and a hunch is a hunch."

"What's the matter with Joe?"

"Same trouble. He's got a horse running in the Holly stakes. Sixth race. A horse named Juan. He's been watching him all year. A long shot."

"Well, I'm sure I don't know why the men come out to the track if it's going to make them so unhappy," Mrs Dexter said. "Oh, I forgot. I've a very important message for you from Napier.

Terribly important. I wanted to tell you at lunch but I missed you. I went out to the spa with Napier this morning. And—"

Joe and Charles returned to the table. They sat down. They were very unhappy.

"Well, to get back to Napier," Mrs Dexter said. "I went out to the spa with him this morning and—"

"There they go," Charles groaned. He was leaning forward a little as if his stomach pained him.

The sweet, desultory fall of hoofs came to them there as the entries filed up from the paddock. The jockeys' silks burned in the sun.

"Which is he?" Mrs Dexter asked. "Which is he?"

"Number four," Joe said.

"That black one? Well, I don't think Crepe is an awfully good name for that horse. Do you, Charles? Do you think they ought to name a black horse Crepe? Why, I think that's gruesome."

"That's not Crepe," Charles said. For one of the few times in his life he spoke to his wife with impatience. "That's Casanova. The one with my money. Crepe is the bay. Number six."

"Oh, I see."

Checked, bridling, the entries paraded up by the clubhouse. They turned and cantered over toward the barrier.

"Well, as I was saying," Mrs Dexter began again, "I went out to the spa with Napier. He wants to see us all. This afternoon. I told him we'd meet him at the hotel at four. He said—" She stopped speaking when she realized that her rather penetrating voice was falling on an unnatural silence. Everyone was watching the horses. They were at the barrier.

The bell rang. That profound, heartbreaking mutter of *they're off* went up like an articulate roll of thunder and was heard by the farmers cultivating their gardens two miles away. The backstretch smoked, the entries streaking, drumming the loose dirt, going faster than anything you can imagine and somehow not fast enough. The numbers went up: the favorite, a horse named Morristown, Crepe, and then Casanova. At the far turn a horse named Battlebridge came up.

Charles said nothing. His hat was drawn down over his eyes. At the turn the favorite rode way out and then it was a horse named Lairdson, Crepe, Casanova, and Battlebridge. Then Lairdson lost out and it was Crepe, Casanova, with Crepe on the rail, and then it was Crepe and Battlebridge, with Casanova nearly seven lengths behind, and then it was Crepe.

The excited roar of the crowd died down into a few heated arguments. A silence settled over the Dexters' table. Charles was staring into his empty glass. Joe was examining his shoes. Lila looked sick. Mrs Dexter was the only one who seemed unconcerned, but it was a long time before even she spoke. "Well, I've won twenty dollars," she said quietly. "Here, Joe, take my ticket and get the money. Whiskey for the men," she told a waiter, "and I'll have vermouth."

When the drinks were finished, Charles and Mrs Dexter left. Lila promised to leave after the next race and meet them at the hotel. It was not until they were alone together in the taxi that Mrs Dexter asked Charles how much he had lost.

"A thousand. All we have. I don't know how we'll pay the hotel bill. Poor Lila. We'll have to go back tomorrow. Poor kid."

"I have my jewelry."

"Yes."

They rode for some time without speaking.

They were both thinking the same thing. She was the one who mentioned it. "There's always Lord Devereaux," she said; "he'll stake us."

"Yes," he said tiredly, "there's always Lord Devereaux."

THEY WERE BACK at the hotel, counting their change, when they heard the metallic sound of a key in the lock. The door shot open, banging the wall, and Lila came in. She looked as if she had been running. Her hair was loose and she was carrying her hat. She ran through the parlor into the bedroom. "I'll go," Mrs Dexter said.

"It's Joe," Lila sobbed. "After you and Dad left we just sat there and had a drink and I made a two-dollar bet on the next race. Then I said I ought to go, and he said all right. Then he said he thought we ought to make it goodbye. He said he was going to leave the track for good, win or lose. He said we wouldn't see each other any more. So then he walked out toward the gates with me. We said goodbye. Out there by the closed paddock. You know. We kissed but then he turned and walked off and I felt as if they were tearing my arm away from me. I didn't know it could be like that. I can't live without him."

Mrs Dexter said nothing. She let her arm rest on her daughter's shoulders. Then she stood and left the room, closing the door after her. She hesitated in the corridor between the parlor and the bedroom. It was the time to make a decision, but she was too bewildered, too stunned, to think. Her hard work had been mistaken and in vain. She was unprepared for this. When she entered the parlor Charles was shouting into the telephone: "I don't care if they haven't run the sixth yet. Get him for me, get Joe for me and tell him to come to Charlie Dexter's hotel. Tell him it's important. No. It's nothing about a horse." He slammed down the receiver.

Fifteen minutes later Joe came into the room. "She's in there," Mrs Dexter said, gesturing toward the bedroom. He went in and she closed the door after him. The telephone began ringing. Charles answered it.

"Lord Devereaux calling on Mr and Mrs Dexter," the clerk said.

"Send him up," Charles said.

They retreated to their chairs and waited. They

heard the creak of the ancient elevator mounting its shaft. They heard a rap on the door. "Come in," Mrs Dexter said. "Oh, Napier!"

Napier stood by the door, waiting for someone to take his hat and stick. Then he placed them on the floor, the hat upside down like a receptacle.

"Don't people ever put ashes in it?" Charles asked.

"In what?"

"In your hat?"

"Mercy no!"

"Oh, stop it, Charles, stop it!" Mrs Dexter said impatiently. "It's the heat," she explained, fanning herself with a handkerchief; "it's the frightful heat. It's made us all ill-tempered. Can I order some iced tea, Napier?"

"Thank you, no," he said. "Never drink it. Frightful stuff. Is Lila here?"

"Lila?" Mrs Dexter asked first herself and then her husband. Her time was up. It was the decision of her life that would have the greatest conse- quences, and the strain of making it told on her face. "Lila? No, she's not here right now." Her voice was lifeless. "She went out for a minute."

She began fanning herself again. In the silence

she heard Joe and Lila's voices from behind the closed door.

"Oh, I wonder where Lila is?" she asked, raising her voice. "She's not exactly punctilious. There's something you ought to know, Napier. I should have told you before. Lila has never been exactly punctilious."

"But I—" Napier began.

"No, no, no," she sang, "don't interrupt me. I feel that I ought to tell you about it. Lila is frequently late. Sometimes as much as a day late. She's not the sort of person you can depend upon. In New York we never know where she is. She's sometimes gone for days at a time. Sometimes for weeks. Last winter she disappeared for three weeks. In January. We never tell the police. That's something you must remember after you're married. Never call in the police. You can't tell where you're going to find her. Frightfully embarrassing."

Charles's face blanched and his mouth hung open at the fabric of lies his pretty wife was spinning. Mrs Dexter had begun to circle the room slowly, picking up and blowing imaginary dust from every loose object she passed. "I've always thought of it as amnesia," she went on, searching her harried imagination for horrors. "Personally, I've always thought of it as amnesia. At least, that's the most discreet way of looking at it. Don't you think? There's nothing hereditary about amnesia. Or is there? Personally, I've always thought of it as amnesia.

"Now when we were playing Reading, Pennsylvania," she said, and her flagging imagination seemed to have taken on new strength, "when we were playing Reading, Pennsylvania, she disappeared for nearly a month. Remember, Charles? We were playing a theatre there called the Opera House. I did a little number with a rose between my teeth. Charles did a buck-and-wing. Did you know Charles can do a buck-and-wing? Or perhaps we haven't told you about our theatrical life. Or have we?"

"You haven't." The voice was the voice of an outraged man.

"Yes," she said tiredly, airily, "we were in the theatre for years and years. Lila was born backstage. In a theatre called the Strand. That was in Omaha, Nebraska. Her middle name is Strand. Lila Strand Dexter. Nice, don't you think? We were playing the intermission at a burlesque house then. Remember my costume, Charles? And that little number I sang." She stood in the center of the floor, swaying a little to some remembered melody.

For all her chattering, her absentmindedness, her indiscriminate collection of friends, no one, until then, could ever have accused Tilly Dexter of anything that was either comic or undignified. She was a woman who cherished her dignity, and now that she was destroying it, it was with a great effort. She took three steps, first to the left, then to the right and made a frank attempt to kick. Her face was flushed with the exertion and her hair was coming loose. She began to sing:

"I'm not too young and I'm not too old,
I'm not too hot and I'm not too cold—"

The door slammed on Lord Devereaux.

IT WAS IN the prolonged silence that followed Lord Devereaux's departure that they became conscious of the silence from the further room.

Lila and Joe had stopped talking. Then Mrs Dexter began to cry. She wept quietly, bitterly. Charles went to her and he felt her thin shoulders shaking under his arm. "There's no reason to cry, Tilly," he said quietly. "She has what she wants. That's what we came for. There's no reason to cry."

He stood and went to the window. The races were over and the crowds in their summer clothes were coming back into town. "Extra! Extra!" a news-boy was crowing. "Long shot takes Holly stakes by four lengths! Juan wins Holly stakes! Extra! Extra! Read all about it!"

Collier's
August 24, 1940

Family Dinner

H E WAS THERE first, a thing that was to be expected. The weekend crowds had gone and had not yet begun to return and there were only a few soldiers in that part of the railroad station that resembles the Baths of Caracalla. He was early; she was on time and at a quarter to one he saw her coming down the escalator. I have never seen her before—he thought—I am a stranger, a drummer waiting for a Baltimore train and is she worth watching or isn't she? They had not seen each other for a month but their meeting was no meeting. It seemed more like the resumption of a quarrel they had left off only a few minutes before.

"This is the last time," he said.

"Oh, all right, all right. Only if she finds out it will kill her, Frank, she'll drop down dead. They'll both drop down dead."

"You've got to tell her."

"I will. Only give me a chance to straighten things out first, will you?"

"Where are you living?"

"East Sixty-seventh Street," she said. "Where are you living?"

"At the club," he said.

They walked down to the lower level and boarded the train. They did not speak again until the train was passing through the badlands outside Newark. Then he picked up her hand and examined a bracelet she was wearing. "You shouldn't wear such showy jewelry," he said; "it makes you look like a gypsy."

"You shouldn't wear gray," she said, "it makes you look bilious." Then she began to laugh. "I'll never forget the time you pretended to commit suicide," she said. "Every time I see you I think of that." She rested her forehead on one hand, laughing. "I'll never forget that, not if I live to be a hundred. I can still see you lying on the . . ." He got up and went to the platform to smoke a cigarette and remained there until the train pulled into Montclair.

She had not told them when she was coming so

there was no one at the train. Morrisey, the old cab driver, came up. "Hullo, Mrs Minot, hello, Mr Minot. Coming home for a change? Well, it's good to see you. I see your father nearly every morning, Mrs Minot." He opened the cab door and they got in.

They stopped at the house and Frances waited while Frank paid the fare. "I want to go back on the six-thirty," she whispered when the cab had driven off, and then she took his arm for the walk up the path. Mr Godfrey opened the door for them before they had time to ring. He embraced his daughter with deep affection and shook hands cordially with his son-in-law.

Mr Godfrey was a straight, handsome man in his sixties, dressed for Sunday dinner in clothing that looked a shade too clean and too well-pressed. "Well, how are things in New Yack?" he asked. He had come from Massachusetts many years ago but he still spoke with a sharp seaboard accent. While Frank was taking off his coat, Jeannette—Frances's niece—came running into the hall and kissed her aunt. She shook hands with Frank, made a curtsy and thundered back into the living room.

Then Mrs Godfrey came out of the kitchen and embraced them both. She was a comfortable, openhearted woman who tried to restrain her easy affection but when she put her arms around Frances she began to cry. She forced her wet face into a smile and stepped back to admire the dress her daughter was wearing, and although it needed no adjustment she gave several touches to the neckline as though Frances were still a child. With her arms around their waists she led them into the living room where her other, plainer daughter, Priscilla, and her husband, Ralph, were drinking sherry. "I have all my children now," Mrs Godfrey said. "Nothing makes me so happy. This is what I live for." She poured Frances and Frank a glass of sherry and forced some crackers on them.

Ralph greeted Frank heartily and began to tell him about his affairs. "We didn't get started until after twelve because we slept late this morning," he said. "My partner called me up last night from Houston, Texas. On the telephone.

"His voice was as clear as a bell," Ralph said. "We're going to meet him in Miami in February. Priscilla and I are going down. We're going to leave Jeannette with her grandmother."

"I want to go to Florida," Jeannette said.

"You can't go, sugar," Ralph said, and he roughed her yellow hair with his hand. "Maybe next year."

"I think everything's on the table," Mrs Godfrey said. "I'll go and see." She called to them from the dining room and asked Ralph to bring in the chair and the sofa cushions for Jeannette to sit on. Frank carried the chair and Ralph brought along the cushions and they made the child comfortable between her mother and Frank. Mrs Godfrey lighted the four candles on the table with a kitchen match. Mr Godfrey carved a few slices off the roast beef and put them onto a plate with vegetables. The maid carried this out to the kitchen for herself. Then Priscilla noticed the bracelet Frances was wearing.

"Frank gave it to me for my birthday," Frances explained. She unclasped the bracelet and passed it across the table to her sister.

"Oh, I think it's beautiful," Priscilla said. "Do you mind if I try it on? If you ever think of marrying again, Frank, I wish you'd put me on your list. Ralph never gives me jewelry."

"We can't have everything, dear," Ralph said.

"It's the most beautiful thing I've ever seen," Mrs Godfrey said quietly; then the bracelet was passed to her and she fastened it on Frances's wrist again.

"Have you seen any of the new plays?" Priscilla asked her sister.

"We haven't gone to the theatre much this year," Frances said. "We went to the Stork Club the night before last. We sat beside Luise Rainer."

"What does she look like?" Priscilla asked Frank.

"I didn't see her," Frank said. By that time everyone had been served. The Godfreys ate industriously and without much talk, and a silence, broken only by the noise of china and silver, continued until Mr Godfrey stood again before the roast, brandishing the carving set.

"You'll have another piece of meat, Frances. A little of the gold edge?"

"Oh, no, thank you, Dad. I couldn't eat another thing."

"You'll have another piece of meat, Frank? Mother? . . ." They went quickly through their dessert and when they had extinguished their cigarettes in their coffee cups they started back for the living room. Ralph returned the sofa cushions his daughter had been sitting on and Mr Godfrey replaced the chair. Mrs Godfrey took Frank's arm as he was leaving the room and held him back a little.

"How are you, dear?" she asked.

"Fine."

"You look a little troubled."

"I can't imagine why."

"Frances is looking awfully well. You take such good care of her, Frank." As she came into the living room she said, "Now let's have some music, Priscilla."

As a result of those afternoons Frank would associate Chopin with indigestion for the rest of his life; but the music then seemed pleasant to him and a sudden relief. Mrs Godfrey watched Priscilla with a half-smile on her face. Mr Godfrey also smiled at the evidence of the advantages he had been able to give his daughter. Ralph listened carefully, looking now and then in Jeannette's direction to make sure that she was quiet. Frances watched the carpet and the clock.

Surfeited with food, with work, with the burdens

of their lives, they sat stiffly in their uncomfortable chairs as though the music were a kind of imprisonment. In the heaviness of the atmosphere, the steam heat and the smells of cooking, the arpeggios seemed incredibly light and ascendent and because Frank supposed that Chopin was French he remembered then an early summer morning, five years ago, when he and Frances had bicycled into Avignon and some soldiers called after her: *"Hé, la blonde, hé la blonde. . . . "*

The music ended suddenly. They clapped and Priscilla began to play the "Moonlight Sonata." Frank noticed Mr Godfrey signaling to him. The two men got up stealthily and left the living room for the dining room where Mr Godfrey poured out two small drinks of brandy. Ralph's exclusion from these meetings was a rudeness Frank had never understood. They could hear the music distinctly from where they sat. Outside it was growing dark.

"Good to have you with us," Mr Godfrey whispered.

"Good to be here."

"Happy days."

"Happy days."

"Priscilla plays very well, don't you think?"

"Very well."

"I wonder how far she would have gone if she had taken it up seriously."

"There are so many good pianists."

"Yes, that's what they say. . . ."

They had gone over that dialogue more times than he could remember and the tenderness Frank felt for the other man still kept it from seeming ridiculous. There was the harsh rattle of applause again, a sudden silence and then Jeannette's unpleasant voice.

"How lovely is the evening," she sang.

"When all the bells are ringing.

"Ding-dong, ding-dong . . ."

THERE WAS MORE applause and then another piece. Frank and Mr Godfrey finished their brandies. When they returned to the living room everyone was standing around the piano looking at a photograph album. "You'll want to see this, Frank," Mrs Godfrey called. "Come and stand by me. This is a photograph we took of Frances in 1926. Would you know her?"

"I think I would," Frank said.

"This is one we took at the Blaisdells' picnic. She was only fourteen years old then. Her hair was so light. That Wiley boy was sparking her. He's the one on the left beside Aunt Louise. Doesn't he look funny in that bathing suit? That's the costume she wore when she was in the *Cradle Song*."

"You know, Mother dear," Frances said softly, "we've got to go back. It's six o'clock." She slipped one arm around her mother's waist.

"Oh, but you can't go yet," Mrs Godfrey cried. The forced, empty smile on her face looked like fright.

"Maybe they have to go, Mother," Mr Godfrey said.

"We have to be in town at seven," Frances said.

"Are you sure you don't want something to eat before you go?"

"Of course not, dear. We just had our dinner."

"Do you want to take some roast beef back with you?"

"No, thanks."

"Some of that cake?"

"No, thank you, no."

They made their farewells on the porch, looking like one of those pathetic and bewildered groups you sometimes see at country railroad stations or in the waiting rooms of city hospitals. Ralph drove them to the train. The train was crowded and they took seats in different coaches. Frank went up to the platform to smoke and standing there he could see her hat and her shoulders, but he left the train as soon as the doors were opened and he did not see her again.

Collier's
July 25, 1942

The Opportunity

MRS WILSON SOMETIMES thought that her daughter Elise was dumb. Elise was her only daughter, her only child, but Mrs Wilson was not so blinded by love that the idea that Elise might be stupid did not occasionally cross her mind. The girl's father had died when she was eight, Mrs Wilson had never remarried, and the girl and her mother lived affectionately and closely. When Elise was a child, she had been responsive and lively, but as she grew into adolescence, as her body matured, her disposition changed, and some of the wonderful clarity of her spirit was lost. At sixteen she seemed indolent, and to have developed a stubborn indifference to the hazards and rewards of life. She was a beautiful girl with dark hair and a discreet and striking grace, but Mrs Wilson sometimes thought sadly that there was a discrepancy between Elise's handsome brow and what went on behind it. Her face and her grace were almost never matched by anything she had to say. She would sit for an hour on the edge of her bed, staring at nothing. "What are you thinking about?" Mrs Wilson would ask; "what's on your mind, Elise?" Elise's answer, when she made it, was always the same. "Nothing. I don't know. I wasn't thinking about anything."

Mrs Wilson worked as a secretary. They lived in a three-room walk-up over a grocery store. They were poor. Elise, in her first two years at high school, had got brilliant grades, and Mrs Wilson had hoped to get her a college scholarship, but in her third year Elise's grades slumped, and she barely passed into the senior class. She didn't seem to mind. She said she didn't care. Mrs Wilson gave up the idea of a scholarship and decided that Elise should take a commercial course in her senior year and go to work when she graduated. She made the decision regretfully but with a clear eye on the future, for Mrs Wilson had no rich relatives or any other expectations of help beyond her own ability to work and save. She told Elise her plans, early in the summer after school had closed.

"I really didn't want to go to college," Elise said.

"Well I'm glad it isn't too much of a disappointment, dear," Mrs Wilson said. "I'll go over next week and see about enrolling you in the commercial course."

"I don't want to take a commercial course," Elise said.

"Why not, dear?"

"It would be a waste of my time," Elise said. "Why should I take a commercial course? What good would that do me? I'm going to be an actress. A commercial course would be a waste of time. I'm going on the stage."

"When did you decide this?"

"Oh, a long time ago," Elise said.

Mrs Wilson struggled to hold her temper. She felt that she had had more than her share of loneliness and hard work since her husband's death, and to have these burdens increased with the worries of an indolent and stage-struck girl made her feel desperate and tired. She waited until this feeling had passed. Then she began, patiently, to describe to the girl the difficulties of the theatre. Thousands of experienced, beautiful, and talented

actresses were out of work. Even those who did
work, didn't work often, and only a few of the
thousands in the profession made an annual salary as big as a file clerk's. When Mrs Wilson had
finished, Elise said nothing.

"Well, what are you thinking, dear?" Mrs Wilson
asked. "What's on your mind?"

"Nothing," Elise said. "I don't know. I wasn't
thinking about anything." She yawned. "I guess
I'll go to bed." She kissed her mother good night,
and went into her room. It also seemed to Mrs
Wilson that Elise needed a lot of sleep. She
couldn't remember the needs of her own youth,
but it seemed to her that Elise spent an awful lot
of time sleeping.

ELISE SPENT A month in the country with her
grandmother that summer. This was her vacation.
When she returned to New York in August, she
took up again the job as baby-sitter that had oc-
cupied most of her spare time during the winter,
and all of her time when she was not in school.
She worked regularly for a young couple named

Cogswell, who had two girls and a baby boy. She took the children to the park, gave them their meals, their baths, and if the Cogswells were having guests for cocktails, as they often did, she stayed with the children until the guests had left. She gave half of the salary she got for this to her mother and spent the other half on orange drinks, frankfurters, candy bars, ice cream, rental-library fees, and silver bracelets. She had twenty-two silver bracelets and dreamed of having fifty. When she had finished at the Cogswells, she would walk slowly home. She would eat supper with her mother and sometimes, as the autumn approached, Mrs Wilson would bring up the question of Elise's future.

"Elise, dear, I wish you'd think seriously about taking that commercial course," she'd say.

"But Mother. I've told you that I think it's a waste of time," Elise would say quietly. Then Elise would disappear into her room and, it seemed to Mrs Wilson, into the dark continent of adolescence. There was an Amherst and a Williams pennant over her bed, but the other walls were covered with photographs that she had cut out of *Life* magazine. This gallery depressed Mrs

Wilson. If the pictures had made any sense, or if there had been any connection between one picture and another, she wouldn't have minded so much, but the pictures had been chosen indiscriminately, or along mysterious lines of discrimination. Overlapping a portrait of a Doberman pinscher was a picture of some Chinese refugees walking along a bank of the Yangtze river. Next to these was a picture of the Casino at Nice, Rex Barney, a wedding in Chicago, the damage done by a tornado in Oklahoma, and the coronation of a chief in Africa.

LATE IN AUGUST the Cogswells had a large cocktail party, and Elise stayed late at their apartment that day. At seven o'clock, she took the children into the living room to say good night to their parents and the guests, and when she had returned with them to the nursery, she thought she heard herself being discussed by one of the guests. Elise was changing the baby's diaper when Mrs Cogswell came into the nursery and said that one of the guests was a theatrical agent, and that she wanted to talk with Elise. Mrs Cogswell was very excited at this turn of events, but Elise finished folding and pinning the diaper before she spoke. "All right," she said.

She returned to the living room with Mrs Cogswell and was introduced to Gloria Hegel, the agent. The party was breaking up. Miss Hegel drew Elise down beside her on the sofa and stared at her intently. "Darling," she said. "Tom Leary has just written a new play and the lead is for a girl of about your age and they've been trying to cast it all summer and they haven't been able to find anyone—*anyone*. I know what they want. I've talked with Tommy, and the minute I saw you walk into this room I knew you were it. Now, have you ever thought of going on the stage?"

"I've decided that I would," Elise said.

"Have you ever had any experience?"

"No."

"Can you come down to my office tomorrow afternoon?"

"You'll have to ask Mrs Cogswell."

"Of course you can," Mrs Cogswell said. "Isn't this exciting?"

Miss Hegel gave Elise her address and made an appointment with her for three, and after she had left, both the Cogswells told Elise that she was the biggest agent in New York, and they named six or seven movie stars she had handled. Mr Cogswell mixed another shaker of drinks, and the couple seemed more excited than the girl. When Elise's work was finished, she walked home slowly and told her mother the news.

"I may have a job, Ma," she said.

"That's nice," Mrs Wilson said. "Baby-sitting?"

"On the stage," Elise said.

"Now, you've got to get this idea of going on the stage out of your head," Mrs Wilson said.

"But this agent said that she thought she could get me a part," Elise said quietly. "I didn't ask her. She asked me. Her name is Gloria Hegel. She's kind of funny looking. She was at the Cogswells. I'm going to see her tomorrow."

"Well, there's nothing to get excited about, is there?" Mrs Wilson said.

"I'm not excited," Elise said.

The Opportunity

FOR HER INTERVIEW with Miss Hegel, Elise dressed, as she dressed for everything, in a long, voluminous skirt and a pair of worn ballet slippers. She put on all her silver bracelets, and if it had been raining, she would have put on her head a scarf that had ELISE ELISE ELISE ELISE written on it. It wasn't raining. It was a hot day at the end of summer. One of Elise's many physical gifts was that she could appear cool, even in the most sustained heat. When she came into Miss Hegel's office that afternoon, she looked composed and fresh. Miss Hegel was wearing a hat and talking on the telephone. She made a broad gesture of welcome to Elise, scowled at the telephone, and nodded for Elise to sit down. She made it clear that Elise stood much higher in her estimation than the person she was talking with. "I know, darling, I know," she kept saying impatiently into the telephone, "I know, darling, but I'm busy now and you'll have to call me later." She slammed the receiver into its cradle and swung around to Elise.

"I have the most exciting news for you, darling," she said. "I talked with Harry Belber this morning and I told him about you, and you're just what they want. I was afraid the fact that you don't have any experience would count against you, but Harry told me that it doesn't make any difference, that Ben Traveler would rather teach a beginner what to do than teach somebody what not to do, and that what they're looking for is the kind of fresh, unspoiled charm you have. They want me to bring you over to the theatre this afternoon." She glanced at her watch. "Of course, we can't be sure you're going to get the part, but there's an awfully good chance you will and this office is one hundred percent behind you. The play is going to be a hit—I know that—it's just what the audiences want, and if you get the part we'll sign a year's contract and after you've been on Broadway for a year I'll take you out to the coast. Cigarette?"

"No, thank you," Elise said. "I don't smoke."

"The play is called *The Devil's Eye* and it's by Tom Leary," Miss Hegel said. "He has had eight hits on Broadway and twenty-six screen credits. You don't have to worry about your author. Ben Traveler is going to direct it, and I guess I don't have to tell you that he's one of the best-known directors on Broadway. Harry Belber's going to produce it. He has never produced a show before, but his grandfather left him millions and millions of dollars from that abrasive business and the production is budgeted at a hundred and fifty thousand. After all, a producer never does anything but send out for sandwiches, anyhow. When you go over to the theatre this afternoon they'll expect you to walk on, and if they like your looks they'll ask you to read a few lines. Do you think you'll have any trouble? Stage fright, I mean?"

"No," Elise said.

"Good, darling," Miss Hegel said. She settled back in her chair and gave Elise a thorough, nearly accusatory look. "Your hair's all right," she said, "and Jack's going to be over at the theatre to put on your make-up. Let's go."

WHEN THEY GOT to the theatre, Elise was surprised to find a crowd in the lobby. At first she thought that there must be a matinee and that the men and women had come out for a cigarette, and then she realized that they, like herself, were looking for work. An elderly man was speaking to the crowd. "Mr Belber and Mr Traveler are terribly sorry," he was saying, "but all the parts for this one are cast." The crowd began to turn away. "Mr Belber and Mr Traveler want to thank you very much, and they're both very sorry that you've come all the way over here for nothing, but all the parts for this one are cast. Mr Belber and Mr Traveler want to thank you very much . . ." The crowd started out, and Miss Hegel took Elise into the theatre.

The auditorium was dark, and except for three men she could see sitting in the front row, the place was empty. The stage was set and lighted for a play that was still running, and the sense of contrived illusion, given by the darkness and the lighted set and the sense that to be in a theatre at that unusual hour was a privilege, a mark of importance, pleased and excited the girl. The set was familiar. It represented a comfortable living room. The furniture was covered with sheets, as if the tenants had gone away for the summer, but the rest of the set was as it would be that night when the audience arrived. Miss Hegel led Elise down a side aisle and through a box to the back of the stage. Waiting behind the set were thirty or forty more actresses, and adding these to the crowd in the lobby, Elise had not known there were so many. A man put on her stage make-up in a dressing room, and she returned to wait with the others. As their names were called, they would walk onto the set. The conversations they had with the powers in the front row didn't vary much. "How do you do, Miss Hodge," the director would say. "We're very glad you came over, but I'm afraid there's nothing for you in this. Thank you very much. How do you do, Miss Beverly. We're very glad you came over, but I'm afraid there's nothing for you in this. Thank you very much. How do you do, Miss Griswold . . ."

The outward indifference with which they took their chance and lost was the first that Elise had seen of the theatre's good humor, and the openness with which these women talked to her while she waited was her first experience with the theatre's peculiar kindliness. Then it was her turn. She walked onto the stage. The number of bright, colored lights directed on it surprised her. She looked out into the dark auditorium, but with the light against her eyes she could see no one there.

"How do you do, Miss Wilson," someone said. "We're very glad you came over. Now, will you please come forward a little? The light's better there. Thank you. How old are you, Miss Wilson?"

"Sixteen."

"Have you ever had any experience?"

"No."

"Would you take a few steps, please."

"Yes." She walked toward the wings. She could see Gloria smiling broadly.

"Thank you, thank you," the voice from the dark said. "Now will you say something for us, Miss Wilson."

"What would you like me to say?"

"Anything."

"'The quality of mercy is not strained,'" she said. "'It droppeth as the gentle rain from heaven upon the . . .'"

"That's enough, thank you, Miss Wilson. I think we've heard enough. Now I wonder if you'd go through a scene for us? Gloria has a copy of the script. You can look it over, and in about fifteen minutes we'll want you to come on again and go through a speech."

"All right," she said.

"Thank you very much."

She walked off the set. Gloria embraced her excitedly and led her back to one of the dressing rooms. The speech she was expected to read was made by a young girl to her stepmother. In it, she refused to enter into a marriage her step-mother had arranged for her. "You can't make me marry Rickey," it began. "No one can make me marry Rickey . . . ." Elise read it once to her-self, and then read it twice aloud to Gloria. Then she was called back to the stage, and she walked onto the set.

"Where shall I stand?" she asked.

"A little more toward center."

"Here?"

"That will do."

"Shall I begin now?"

"Yes."

"You can't make me marry Rickey," she began. "No one can make me marry Rickey . . . ."

When she had finished the speech she relaxed, as if reading it had taken something out of her. She looked toward the dark. From there she heard excited whispering, in which the words "wonderful, wonderful" were repeated. Then she saw Gloria beckoning to her wildly from the wings, and she walked off the set. "They love you!" Gloria said. "They love you; you've got the part. They want to see you in the office." Backstage was empty, Elise noticed. All the others had gone. Miss Hegel led her up some back stairs to an office, and Mr Belber, Mr Traveler, and Mr Leary came in.

The three men seemed to her kind, witty, and rich. Their conservative clothes, their gray hair, and the heavy-framed glasses they all wore made her think of the directors of a trust company. When the introductions were finished, they told her they wanted her for the part and would give her a copy of the play to read that night. Rehearsals would begin in three days. They would discuss the contract with Miss Hegel in the morning and sign it at noon. Miss Hegel would have to get Elise an Equity card and see about entering her in the professional children's school. They agreed to meet at noon, and Elise and Miss Hegel left and got a taxi.

"I'm not going to sign a run-of-the-play contract," Miss Hegel said, as they drove across town. "I'm only going to let them have you for a year. Then I'll take you out to the coast for two years. Then back to Broadway for another play. Then back to the coast. Then back here for a musical. Can you sing? Can you dance?"

"Not much," Elise said.

"Well, you can learn," Gloria said. "Back here for a musical with a television show on the side, and then back to the coast again, and you won't even be twenty-three years old." She began to talk about hundreds and thousands of dollars and, absorbed in these calculations, she said goodby to Elise absentmindedly. Elise walked home.

IT WAS AFTER six, and Mrs Wilson was waiting. "I think I've got it, Ma," Elise said. "Miss Hegel's going to ask for five hundred a week, but she doesn't think I'll get more than three-fifty. They gave me a copy of the play. I've got to read it to-night."

Mrs Wilson sat down. If the poor woman had

ever allowed herself to expect anything, the shock might not have been so great, but because she had contented herself with the thought of a hard life, the prospects of Broadway and Hollywood staggered her. Elise got her mother a glass of water and sat on the arm of her chair until she had recovered.

"Well, I thought we might go out tonight and have dinner in a restaurant for a celebration," Mrs Wilson said, "but if you have to read the play tonight I guess we'd better put off our celebration. I suppose there'll be a lot of work to it, as well as money and excitement."

Mrs Wilson cooked the dinner, and when they had finished and washed the dishes, Elise went into her room to read the play, and Mrs Wilson sat down with some sewing. She was intensely excited, but she was proud of the composure they were both showing. If anyone should look into their apartment, they would not know that night was unlike any other. It was hot. All the familiar sounds of that neighborhood on a late summer night came through the open windows. From the other room, she could hear Elise turning the pages of the play. She had been sewing and the girl had been reading for about three hours, when she heard Elise get up from her desk and come to the door. She looked up and saw that Elise had been crying.

"Is it a sad play, dear?" Mrs Wilson asked.

"No." Elise ran to her mother, knelt on the floor beside her chair, and put her face in her mother's lap. She began to cry again.

"But what's the matter, dear?" Mrs Wilson asked. "Tell me. Tell me what's the matter?"

"It stinks," Elise said.

"What do you mean, dear?"

"I mean the play stinks," Elise cried. She lifted her swollen face and looked at her mother. "I can't be in it, I just can't be in it, Mother. I wouldn't be in such an awful play, I don't care how much they paid me. It's worse than any movie I ever saw; it's even worse than the comic books. It stinks." She put her face in her mother's lap and sobbed for a while. Then she lifted her head again.

"You see, it's about this old actress who lives in a big country house in the fashionable part of Maryland," she said. "That's what it says right in the play. 'In the fashionable part of Maryland.'"

Well, I'm her stepdaughter and she wants me to marry a rich man named Rickey, and I want to marry a farmer named Joel. And in the end it turns out that Joel was rich all the time." She sobbed a little at the thought of this; then went on: "On top of this, there's this zany family living in the house, the same zany family that they've had in every play and movie since the flood. There's a crazy old man in the cellar who thinks he's making atomic bombs, and a punchy prize fighter who thinks he's Thomas Edison and there's an Englishman with a monocle and a cane that explodes and a parrot that talks with a French accent and in one scene I have to come out of a grandfather clock making noises like a cuckoo."

"Well, as you describe it, it doesn't sound very good, I'll admit," Mrs Wilson said judiciously, "but do you think we're the ones to judge whether or not a play is good? After all, Mr Leary has written eight very successful plays, and you told me Miss Hegel said that Mr Traveler had directed many successful plays. Surely Mr Belber wouldn't want to invest a hundred and fifty thousand dollars in something that hasn't any merit."

"I don't understand that," Elise said. "I just

know the play stinks."

"But how can you be so sure, dear?" Mrs Wilson asked.

"I can be sure of what I like and what I don't like, can't I?" Elise asked. "I'm not going to come out of a grandfather clock making noises like a cuckoo for anybody. I don't like the play. I don't want to be in it."

"Perhaps if you sleep on it . . ."

"I don't have to sleep on it."

"Well, let's go to bed and sleep on it," Mrs Wilson said. "We're both tired."

But Mrs Wilson couldn't sleep. She didn't know what to do. She couldn't force the girl to take the part, but at the same time, to see inexperience refuse a promise of so much money and pleasure gave her a painful wrench. She heard Elise sigh in the dark, and thinking that the girl might be wakeful, too, she went into her room—but Elise, as soon as she had got into bed, had fallen into the deep sleep of youth. Mrs Wilson noticed on the walls photographs of Rex Barney, the late Mrs Harvey Cushing, Henry Wallace, Valentina, Montgomery Clift, Stanton Griffis, and Jackie Robinson.

In the morning, Mrs Wilson left for her office without waking Elise, so that she would not be tempted to influence the girl's decision. Elise would have to decide, and Mrs Wilson wanted, if she could, to keep out of it; but her curiosity and suspense increased as the morning went on, and at ten o'clock she called the apartment and asked Elise if she had made up her mind. "I made up my mind last night," Elise said. Then Mrs Wilson went back to her shorthand notes and her typewriter, her posture chair and her green steel desk, with the realization that she would spend most of the rest of her life in their company. She could expect a pension when she was a white-haired woman of sixty-five. Perhaps then she could retire modestly to New Jersey. She was thankful that the span of hopeful excitement had been so brief.

ELISE'S APPOINTMENT WAS for noon. When she got down to the theatre, Mr Belber, Mr Traveler, and Mr Leary were waiting. Gloria Hegel was there. As soon as Elise stepped into the office, Gloria began to talk. Elise didn't have a chance to say anything until she'd finished. Then she spoke.

"I can't sign the contract," she said.

"What do you mean, darling, what do you mean you can't sign it?" Gloria asked. "I've been over this contract with a fine-tooth comb and you couldn't do any better. You couldn't get a better contract anywhere."

"I don't want to sign it," the girl said.

"But why, darling, why?"

"I read the play last night. I don't want to be in it."

"Do you know anything about this, Gloria?" the producer asked.

"I don't know what's in her head," Gloria said. "I don't know what she's talking about."

"I just don't want to be in it," Elise said.

"If you don't want to be in it, you don't have to be in it," the playwright said. He got her meaning long before the others.

"Now just a minute, Tom," Mr Belber said. "Take it easy."

"If she doesn't want to be in my play, she doesn't have to be in my play," Tom Leary shouted. "I've never seen such effrontery. I never wanted her for the part, anyhow. She's too young. She hasn't had any experience. She's too tall."

"Shut up, Tom," the producer said. Then he turned to Elise. "I don't understand you, Miss Wilson," he said quietly. "Is there something about the contract that isn't satisfactory or is there something, some line in your part that you want changed?"

For the first time during the proceedings the girl seemed to lose her poise. She sat stiffly at the table with her hands folded and her head down, and it cost her an effort to speak.

"It just isn't one speech, Mr Belber," she said. "It's the whole play. I don't like it."

"If she doesn't want to be in my play, she doesn't have to be in my play," Leary shouted. "Get her out of here. Get somebody else. Get the brat out of here. I've got sensibilities just the same as she has. Telephone Hollywood. Get Dolores Random. Get anybody. Get her out of here."

Elise stood. They were all watching. "I'm sorry it turned out this way," she said. "It was very good of you to offer me the chance." She opened the door and went out. Gloria followed and stopped her in the hall. "Is this really what you mean, darling?" she asked. "Are you really turning down this job because you think it isn't any good?"

"Yes," Elise said.

"You little punk," Gloria said. Elise started down the stairs. Gloria shouted after her, "You brat, you baby-sitter, you damned fool."

Elise telephoned Mrs Cogswell from a drugstore and asked if she could come back to work. Mrs Cogswell was delighted. An hour later, Elise was absentmindedly pushing a baby carriage down First Avenue, eating a strawberry ice-cream cone, and smiling at the delivery boys from the grocery store.

Either through forgetfulness or disappointment, Elise never mentioned her experience in the theatre again. But Mrs Wilson couldn't put the experience out of her mind as easily as her daughter, and she began to read eagerly the theatre page of the morning paper in order to follow the fortunes of the play.

The beginning of rehearsals was announced. Elise's part was taken by someone from Hollywood. When the company went to Wilmington for the opening, Mrs Wilson thought of the train ride that she and Elise might have taken, their hotel suite there, and the excitement of an opening. A week later, when the company went to Philadelphia, she made the trip vicariously. She had never been to Philadelphia, but her vision of that city was clear. A week after the opening in Philadelphia, she went to Times Square and bought a trade paper to read a review of the play. It was late and the sidewalk was crowded, but she opened the paper, standing in the middle of the sidewalk, and read the review in the light from the newsstand.

SCORN, RIDICULE, ABUSE, and disgust were heaped on the playwright and his associates, but this vituperation was, in a sense, wasted, for at the bottom of the notice Mrs Wilson read that the play had closed in Philadelphia after five performances. Mr Belber was returning to his grandfather's abrasive business, and Mr Traveler and Mr Leary had gone to their farms. She read the review twice to make sure, and then threw the paper into an ashcan and took a subway home. Elise was sitting in her room, surrounded by her pictures.   A text on double-entry bookkeeping was open in front of her, but she wasn't studying, she was staring at nothing.   Mrs Wilson looked at her daughter with profound love, for she knew that there was some connection between the beauty of the girl's face and the beauty of her judgments.

Cosmopolitan
December, 1949